MOSI'S
WAR

Also by Cathy MacPhail

Run, Zan, Run
Missing
Bad Company
Dark Waters
Fighting Back
Another Me
Underworld
Roxy's Baby
Worse Than Boys
Grass
Out of the Depths
Secret of the Shadows

The Nemesis Series:

Into the Shadows
The Beast Within
Sinister Intent
Ride of Death

MOSI'S WAR

CATHY MACPHAIL

BLOOMSBURY

LONDON NEW DELHI NEW YORK SYDNEY

Bloomsbury Publishing, London, New Delhi, New York and Sydney

First published in Great Britain in May 2013 by Bloomsbury Publishing Plc
50 Bedford Square, London WC1B 3DP

A CIP catalogue record for this book is available from the British Library

ISBN 978 1 4088 1 2723

MIX
Paper from
responsible sources
FSC® C020471

Typeset by Hewer Text UK Ltd, Edinburgh
Printed and bound in Great Britain by CPI Group (UK) Ltd, Croydon CR0 4YY

1 3 5 7 9 10 8 6 4 2

www.bloomsbury.com

For Hamza, with thanks

It was the moving beam of light that caught Patrick's eye. He wouldn't even have glanced out of the landing window if it hadn't been for that sudden, darting flash of light. It wasn't as if there was anything to see out there. A vista of high-rises blocked out anything resembling a view. But the sun came out of the clouds and caught something and for just a second sent a firefly of light dancing across the walls. He took a few steps towards the landing window and he saw it. A figure balancing on the roof of the opposite building. The mesh of steel to stop people from falling, from jumping, had been ripped open and there stood a man, a man who looked more like a puppet than a human being. A second, no, less than a second later the man began to tumble, arms wide, flailing wildly, as if he was trying to catch hold of something, trying to save himself.

Patrick stared. This couldn't be real. It was some kind of joke. Patrick almost laughed as he watched the man falling. Sailing past balcony after balcony, going down floor by floor. Not making a sound.

The world was silent.

It seemed to him that the man was free-falling in slow motion. Patrick was mesmerised by the movement. He didn't even realise he was holding his breath.

Any second and the figure would hit the ground.

Patrick knew he couldn't watch that. He didn't even want to think about it. He drew his eyes away and looked back to the roof. To look at anything other than the man hitting the ground. His legs began to buckle. He drew in a great gulp of air. And the world turned the volume up full blast. There were screams, yells, a car screeching to a halt. He only just stopped himself from screaming. But boys like Patrick didn't scream. Instead, he stumbled back from the window. Stood trembling with his back pressed to the wall. The lift came then. Had it only been seconds since he had pressed the button for it? It seemed ages ago. The doors slid open. Waiting for him. He ignored them. The door to his own flat was on the latch, he always left it on the latch, always getting into trouble for that, from his mum, from his granny. If he went back into the flat, it would make him late for school, again, and then he'd get into more trouble, though he was usually late for school anyway. So why did he care, and why was he even thinking these things?

'Mum . . . Mum . . .' he began to shout as he ran down the hall. 'There's a man . . . he fell . . . he jumped . . . I saw it.'

His mother, sitting in the living room, still in her dressing gown, looked up from her magazine. 'Are you no' away to school yet?'

'Mum, the man fell, I saw him.'

He grabbed her arm, pulled her from the seat.

'What do you think you're playing at, Patrick!' She tried to shake herself free, but he dragged her down the hall, still babbling about what he had seen. Not making any sense. He knew he wasn't making sense. He wanted her to see. He hauled her to the landing window. He dared to look below. Now it was alive with people, swarming like ants around the figure lying on the ground, surrounding him so he was almost blocked from view. In the distance they could already hear the siren of an ambulance, or maybe a police car.

It was as if his mother only just took in what he was saying. 'You saw that man fall?'

He couldn't talk to her. His tongue was stuck to the roof of his mouth. He only nodded.

'Oh, son . . .' And for the first time in an age, his mother hugged him.

Mosi was on the way to school when he heard the commotion. He lived in the same block of flats as Patrick. Three floors below him. But they hardly saw each other except in class. Mosi had left early. He always did. So he had missed the drama that Patrick had witnessed. But bad news travels fast and as he walked he heard snatches of the whispered talk as he passed groups of people gathering on the estate.

'Somebody's fell.'

'It was a man.'

'I heard he jumped.'

'Anybody know who it was?'

'Only one of them asylum seekers.'

Mosi didn't stop. Though he was angry inside. They spoke, some of them, as if the life of an asylum seeker meant nothing. As if asylum seekers didn't feel as other people felt.

He was angry too, more angry, at the man who died. His death would bring the police, publicity, questions.

Hadn't he thought of the other asylum seekers who lived here on this estate? Didn't he consider what his death, his suicide would mean to them? Selfish man. Selfish.

He stopped to watch some boys playing football. Kicking the ball from one to the other. He knew them. They were in his school, some of them in his class. One of the older boys turned to watch him. He smiled. Mosi tried to remember his name.

'Hey, Mosi,' the boy called out to him. Brian . . . that was his name. Always friendly. 'Come on and have a game.'

Two of the other boys stepped forward. 'Do you know the man who topped himself?' one of them shouted.

Mosi didn't answer him. Didn't want to. Didn't want to think of the man who had jumped.

'Did you know him, Mosi?' This time it was Brian who asked.

Again he didn't answer.

Brian called out again. 'Come on, have a kick about before you go to school. It'll be a laugh.'

Another boy pulled him back. 'Leave him be, Brian. That wee Mosi's a weirdo.'

Brian gave him a final wave, then he turned back to his friends. Mosi continued to walk on. What the boy had said hadn't hurt him. Nothing could hurt him now. Anyway, he wasn't a weirdo.

He was something much worse.

2

Patrick began to think it was almost worth seeing a man fall to his death to get the morning off school. That, and being the centre of attention. Well, actually, the dead man was the centre of attention, but Patrick was running a close second. Patrick's mother had dragged him downstairs to the crowd who had all gathered there. She had a habit of dragging him places.

'My boy saw it happen!' she called out dramatically as they emerged from their block. She hauled him into the middle of the crowd. There was a cover over the dead man now. Patrick was glad of that. He tried not to think of what was lying underneath. 'My Patrick saw everything!' she shouted out to anyone who would listen. Everyone did. They all turned. 'Didn't you, Patrick?' She shook him and he nodded. Couldn't stop his head from nodding. He felt like one of those dogs you see in the back of cars. His mother went on. 'He saw it all from up there.' She pointed a scarlet-nailed finger at a window somewhere high in the tower block. 'He was waiting for the lift. He was going to school.'

A big policeman pushed his way through the crowd. Patrick recognised him, and swallowed. This community cop knew Patrick well. 'Ah, Patrick Cleary, you again,' he said.

Patrick was still nodding.

'And you saw this?' He expected the policeman not to believe him, to dismiss him as a liar. Patrick had a reputation for telling stories. But the policeman did a surprising thing. 'Aye,' he went on. 'I can see you saw it. You're as white as a sheet, son.'

'Oh, he's always that colour,' his mother said. 'But even his freckles are white this morning.'

The policeman led Patrick gently to a graffiti-covered bench. Patrick was responsible for most of the graffiti there. Pretty good stuff too, he thought. And he thought again, why am I thinking these things, noticing these thing? But why, at a time like this, am I thinking about graffiti?

'Sit down, Patrick.' The policeman turned to his mother. 'I think your boy could do with a glass of water.'

His mother immediately delegated that task to a woman behind her. 'Could you get my boy a glass of water.' Then she turned to the policeman again. 'He's been in shock since he saw it. Do you think he might need counselling?' Patrick could almost see the wheels of his mother's brain turning.

The policeman ignored her again. He sat down beside Patrick. 'Now, tell me everything you saw.'

He thought he wouldn't find his voice, but he opened his mouth and the words came out, tumbled out, faster and faster, everything he'd seen. It took him longer to say what happened than it took for that man to hit the ground. And Patrick lived those seconds again, seconds that seemed to stretch to an age.

He was interviewed for the television too. The van drew up even before the emergency services had arrived. A reporter pushed his way through, shoving what looked like a hairy lollipop into his face and asking him to describe what he'd seen.

Out it all came again. 'Something made me look over at the other flat, and I saw him.'

'Did he look as if he meant to jump?'

And Patrick saw those terrible moments played out in his mind again.

'Yeah, yeah, he jumped . . . but I think he changed his mind. He jumped, and then, he seemed to panic.' He was breathing hard, on the verge of panic himself, feeling what that man must have felt as he fell. 'I think he changed his mind . . .' he said again.

The policeman had heard enough. He covered the reporter's microphone with his big hand, and held the television crew back. Even told his mother to get out of the way. 'This is too much for a young boy. Get him back home, make him a strong cup of tea. He'll need to give a proper statement later, but I'll make sure he's not bothered till then.'

His mother wasn't too happy about that. She was quite enjoying the 'being bothered' bit. But she took him up to the flat anyway, telling anyone who would listen. 'I would love to stay down here, but . . . you know me, I always put my boy first.'

3

Patrick thought he should have had the whole day off school. He'd seen a suicide, had a big shock. But by the afternoon, and after he had been interviewed by the police again, he was hustled out by his mother. 'You're much better off at school, son. You'll only dwell on it if you stay at home,' she said.

And anyway, this was her bingo afternoon.

Yet, he was glad to be at school. He was greeted like a hero. The main man. He enjoyed the attention, and he found the more he talked, the better he felt. All his friends, especially the boys, wanted him to give a second-by-second description of all he'd seen. And he obliged, dramatising it even more. The man falling through the air, his arms flailing, floating like a puppet.

'Then,' he slapped his hands together, 'blood every-where . . . well, you can imagine.'

Mrs Telford, their form teacher, had allowed him to talk for a while, to let him get it out of his system. Eventually, she stepped in. 'I don't want to hear any more talk of this terrible event. It must have been very traumatic for Patrick.' Patrick didn't look the least bit traumatised. By this time, he was grinning from ear to ear. Mrs Telford looked around the class. Half of them were asylum seekers. 'We are all going to say a prayer for this poor man. We do not know what led him to such a terrible act. Nor should we judge him.'

She closed her hands and bent her head in prayer.

Mosi watched silently. She was a good teacher, Mrs Telford. She knew there were many different faiths in her class. She respected them all. Mosi didn't pray. He had nothing to believe in any more.

He looked at Patrick Cleary. He wasn't praying either. His head was bent, but his eyes were open. He was paler than usual. Mosi could tell that what Patrick had seen had frightened him, though he covered it up with jokes and laughing.

But there was no way Patrick had seen that man hit the ground. Yes, he had watched him fall, but at the moment of impact, he must have turned away, or closed his eyes. Covered his ears to blot out the sound.

Mosi felt weak at the memories he had. And now he did close his eyes. Tried to blot out those memories. Terrible memories. But it was impossible. No way to stop them seeping through the walls of his mind like blood.

No, Patrick Cleary had not seen that man hit the ground.

4

'Did you know him, Mosi?' asked Bliss.

Bliss. Where did she get such a name, Mosi wondered. She was in his class. Long dark hair swept her shoulders, freckles dotted across her nose. His hesitation made her ask him again. 'Did you know him? The man who died?'

Mosi lifted his shoulders. 'He was one of the asylum seekers. It's a big estate, we don't all know each other.'

She tutted. 'I know that, Mosi. I was just asking if you knew him. I heard he was from Africa too.'

'It's a big continent,' was all he said.

Bliss didn't give up. She never did. 'But I mean, if you did know him, that would be really traumatic for you.'

Bliss had heard Mrs Telford use the word 'traumatic' and wanted to use it again. Always trying to impress. Mosi liked her though. It would be hard not to like her. She was always so friendly, so talkative.

Bliss, the name suited her. She'd become something of a heroine after she had arranged with her whole family and all their friends to link arms in front of her best friend Ameira's house and stop a midnight arrest of the whole family. She and Ameira were always together. He was surprised she wasn't beside Bliss now. Ameira's family's asylum application had been upheld. They were now going to be allowed to stay. Ameira gave Bliss all the credit for that. Bliss would be prime minister one day, Mosi was convinced of that. So, why couldn't he smile back at her, answer her, talk to her?

He was afraid. Always so afraid.

'What do you mean, Bliss, traumatic for *him*? I'm the one who saw the man fall.'

Patrick had come up behind her. Bliss hardly turned to him. 'I don't believe you saw anything, Patrick Cleary. You make things up all the time. I remember the story about seeing a UFO.'

'I did see a UFO!' Patrick insisted. 'It was in the sky, and I didn't know what it was. That makes it officially an unidentified flying object – a UFO. So, I did not make that up.'

Bliss rolled her eyes. She looked back at Mosi. 'Back

me up here, Mosi. Do you believe he saw that man falling?'

Mosi looked at Patrick. Patrick had smiling eyes – mischievous, he had heard Mrs Telford call them. Bright blue eyes and a shock of fiery red hair that seemed to drain his face of any colour. He was always up to something, in class or out of school. He was always telling stories. But not this time. 'I believe him,' he said.

'Oh, Mosi, I thought you would know better.' Bliss always talked to him as if they were friends.

Patrick slapped him on the back. 'Thanks, Mosi.'

'I don't know what you're asking him for. He doesn't care about anybody except hisself.' Cody Barr came up beside them. Cody was in their class too but never so friendly as Patrick or Bliss. He didn't like Mosi. Didn't like any of the asylum seekers on the estate. His older brother ran with a gang that had a reputation for causing trouble. But Cody was kept in check in school. Zero tolerance for any kind of racism, or bullying. Signs everywhere. RESPECT.

But once out of school, that didn't matter. Not for Cody. 'A wimp.' He grabbed Mosi by the collar, pulled him towards him, brought his face close to his. 'A real wimp. Know what a wimp is. Do they have that word in your language?' His mouth curled into a sneer. Mosi was sure he must practise that sneer in front of a mirror.

Mosi jerked himself free, stepped back. He never rose to his bait. And that only made Cody angrier.

'Scared o' everything.' Cody spat the words out.

Bliss was scared of nothing. She gave Cody a shove. 'You leave him be or I'll report you.' She turned to Mosi. 'If he gives you any more trouble, you let me know.'

She stomped off towards her best friend, Ameira.

Cody sniggered. 'Oh, fine, now you've got a lassie to protect you. That's what I call a *real* wimp.'

Patrick dragged Cody away. Patrick and Cody were friends, and Mosi could never understand that friendship. 'Leave Mosi be,' he heard Patrick say, 'he never does anybody any harm.' And then, though his voice was soft, he heard Cody's next words, the words he knew he wasn't meant to hear.

'So, are we still on for the night, Patrick?'

5

Mosi's mother looked worried when he got home that day. There was a strong police presence all over the estate. An incident van was parked almost at the entrance to his block of flats. There was a television news van there too. The spot where the man had fallen was marked out with police incident tape.

'They will soon go, *hooyo*,' he tried to assure her.

She shook her head. 'The boy who saw him fall, he lives in this block of flats. Three floors above us. They will be asking questions of everyone here. In case we saw something too. The man came from our country. They will think we might know him.'

He saw her hand shake as she put down his plate of food. His father clasped her fingers. 'It will be all right, Uma. We saw nothing. We know nothing.'

'Did you know this man, *aabo*?' Mosi asked him.

'I talked to people who did. Hassan, his name was. They said he'd been worried, frightened about something, afraid . . .'

'He was being sent back,' his mother said.

'I do not know. But I imagine, yes, he was afraid he was being sent back. His brother disappeared a few weeks ago. Afraid too of being sent back. It is a tragedy.'

'They do not know why he was in that tower block,' his mother said. 'He lived on the other side of the estate.'

His father had an explanation. 'There are many empty flats in that block.' Mosi knew that was true. There had been talk of all these tower blocks being demolished and everyone moved to other parts of the city. His father went on. 'I heard he was stowing food in one of them, so he could hide there if his application for asylum failed.'

His mother let out a long sigh. 'Poor man, how desperate he must have been.'

Mosi still had no sympathy. Why could he not just have disappeared, the way his brother had disappeared? Why such a public death? He hated him for making his mother cry.

Mosi couldn't take his eyes from her. Her mouth trembled. 'Don't be afraid,' he told her. 'They will let us stay here. Daniel has told us that.' Daniel was the man

19

from the YMCA, a kind man, who had helped them since they arrived in Glasgow. He had assured them over and over that their case was almost guaranteed. It was the 'almost' that worried them. He wondered what his mother would do if they were told they were to be sent back. The same as the man today? She had been through so much. She was strong. She had held them all together. But like a strong coat buffeted by the winds she was coming apart at the seams.

And again, he felt only anger at the man who died. How dare he bring this to them?

6

Patrick watched himself on the screen. He'd never been on television before. Did he really look like that? He thought he resembled a lit match. A skinny, pale boy with a head of flaming red hair and freckles. This boy looked nervous. His lips were dry. Patrick watched him run his tongue along them. The boy nodded. 'I saw everything,' he was saying.

Did he really sound like that? Did he really have such a thick Scottish accent? That amazed him as he only ever thought in pure American, like the characters in all the films he watched.

'And where were you when you saw this?'

The boy – he just couldn't think of that boy as himself, as Patrick – the boy pointed up to the tower block. The camera followed his finger. 'I was waiting for the lift. I was going to school.'

'And you saw the whole thing?'

Again he nodded. Patrick remembered thinking he should be telling this story better, describing the man coming over the top of the tower block . . . the silence as he went down . . . the sound of him hitting the ground. He was usually so good at telling stories, but for some reason the right words wouldn't come.

'That must have been quite a shock.'

The journalist had turned to the camera then, Patrick's moment of fame had passed. But Patrick had stopped listening anyway. He wondered if he *had* seen everything. The man had made no sound. All he had seen was a man, his arms flapping like a windmill, falling – and looking as if maybe, just maybe, he'd decided he didn't want to do it after all.

A woman had come to the flat after school, some kind of counsellor, asking if he needed to talk about it. That had made his mother laugh. 'He's been talking about it all day. Can't get him to shut up.'

The woman didn't smile when his mum said that. His mother wasn't taking this seriously enough. But for once, his mum was right. He didn't need to talk to an adult. He had his friends, and they would be happy to listen till he'd talked it out.

The woman had left with a promise, a threat, his mother had called it, of coming back again.

And after she left they had sat together and watched the news, plates of egg and chips on their knees.

'I really think I should have been in that shot with you, Patrick. As your mother, to let people see I was there to support you.' She spoke through a mouthful of chips. 'I mean, I know I gave them permission to film you, but I think I should have been there as well.'

Patrick had to smile at the memory of his mother trying her best to sneak into the shot behind him. She hadn't been quick enough. The interview was over in seconds, and her fifteen minutes of fame had been snatched from her.

She stood up and took his plate from him. 'Now, you don't mind me going out tonight, do you?'

This was unusual. She almost never asked. She went out every night. 'Because I don't mind staying in, son. You have had a very distressing day. And you're my priority.'

He'd heard his granny on the phone ordering her to stay in. 'Don't leave that boy on his own!' she'd shouted. So loud she didn't need a phone. And his mum had assured her she wouldn't. She'd lied. His granny was away on a retreat to the convent at Carfin and wouldn't be back till tomorrow. She'd never find out. Patrick certainly wouldn't tell her.

'Don't be daft, Mum. I'll be fine. Slasher movie on the horror channel.' He grinned at her. His mum was more like a daft big sister really. She'd only been sixteen when he'd been born. She acted as if she was still sixteen. She didn't need much convincing to go out anyway. This was singles night. She would have had a heart attack if he'd asked her to stay in with him.

It was the last thing he wanted anyway. He had things to do. People to meet. His mum was hardly out of the door when Cody called. 'I'll be there in ten minutes,' Patrick said.

Mosi saw the interview on TV too. He watched it with his mother and father in silence.

'The poor boy. What a terrible thing to see,' his mother said.

After speaking to Patrick, the journalist turned to the camera. 'This suicide has focused attention once again on what is happening here for the asylum seekers. Life is hard on this run-down estate. They have to contend with poverty, racist attacks and the fear of being deported.

Although Hassan had still been waiting for a final decision on his asylum application, friends have said he was growing increasingly afraid that he would be sent back. There is an air of tension here on this grim Glasgow estate. We will have to wait to see what the repercussions of this tragic event will be.'

'This means trouble for us,' Mosi's father said.

Mosi agreed. The media made things worse, calling this a grim estate, talking of racist attacks, all this would stir up bad feeling when the majority of them – asylum seekers and the local people – just wanted to keep their heads down. Live quietly. Like Mosi and his parents. And so many of the people here had been helpful and kind. People had offered them furniture, clothes, even food. There were a lot of good people here. But of course, that didn't make such a good story for the media.

Mosi had a tight knot in his stomach. Fear. He recognised it. Had felt it so often before. Something inside him was warning him, bad things were coming. And he didn't know how to avoid them.

After dinner he stood at the window. Looked out over the grey concrete concourse. Black clouds hung so low over the tops of the flats it seemed he could reach out and sink his hands into them. It had begun to rain hard, hitting against the glass like needles. It *was* a grim estate, Mosi agreed, thunder-grey skies, dark stone, cold winds. Not like his own country – cornflower-blue sky, the hot sun.

But there was no homesickness in him. He missed the sun, but that was all. Even hemmed in by all this grey concrete he felt safer here, safer than he could ever remember.

Yet, he knew he wasn't safe. Would he ever be?

A figure ran out of the flats and across the concourse. A boy, his maroon hood pulled over his head. He stopped for a minute waiting for a car to pass before he crossed the street. For a moment he turned and looked up. Almost as if he was looking up at Mosi. Instinctively, Mosi stepped back from the window. The figure was Patrick.

7

'Here's wee Patrick.' Cody was waiting for him by the betting shop. He was surrounded by a group of boys. Some Patrick knew, some he didn't. 'Are you up for it, Patrick?'

Patrick stopped in his tracks, spread his arms wide. 'Ready for anything, me.'

That wasn't completely true. Sometimes Cody got up to things Patrick didn't want to take part in – smashing the chip-shop windows came to mind, or the night they set fire to one of the derelict buildings on the estate. But once he'd started running with Cody's gang, it was hard to say no. And Cody liked him, Patrick was sure of it. He made Cody laugh, and not a lot of people could say that. Most important for Patrick, he had somewhere to go at night, people to share things with. It was always exciting, and Patrick liked exciting.

'We're going to the underpass,' Cody said, pulling Patrick on.

'The underpass?' Patrick was already running alongside him.

'They've cleaned it up. Fresh walls just waiting for us.'

No one ever used the underpass, not at night. It was a short cut under the dual carriageway, leading from the estate to the retail park on the other side of the road. But at night, people would rather take the long way, use the pedestrian crossings, or cross over the bridge. Some people even used the old cemetery that stretched right up behind the estate as a short cut. Safer than the underpass at night-time. The lights were always broken. People had been mugged in there. Only recently a headless cat had been found hanging by its feet, its blood dripping on the ground. That had caused quite a stir. Some people blamed the asylum seekers, especially the African ones. Convinced it had something to do with the voodoo rituals they must have brought from their own countries. Others blamed the gangs of boys who roamed the estate at night, trying to cause trouble. Gangs like Cody's, or his older brother's.

Only one dim light was working. It gave the underpass an eerie glow. But even in this semi-darkness Patrick could see that Cody was right. The underpass had been cleaned up. The walls had been freshly painted white – ready and waiting. Patrick couldn't help feeling excited. There was something about a blank wall that made his heart beat faster. Did that mean there was something wrong with him? He would never tell anyone how much he enjoyed this. He had a talent, he knew he did. A talent his teachers didn't appreciate, a talent his mother had never noticed. But Cody had. That was maybe why he wanted Patrick with him on these nights when they roamed the estate, painting anonymous messages on walls, leaving trails and signs behind them.

Cody turned to him. 'Come on, wee man, do your stuff. Something about that guy falling off the roof, eh? I mean, you saw it. Draw what it looked like, eh? Go on.'

Patrick had already taken out his can, but he felt his hand tremble. He tried to say no. He didn't want to draw that. He wanted to shake the image away. Cody held his gaze, daring him to defy him.

'Got a problem wi' that?'

Patrick hesitated for only a second longer. Cody's minions were all around him, waiting for his answer. He tried to sound cool and casual. 'Who knows better than me what it looked like?'

And he began to spray in swirls and turns. He was impressed himself by the way he could capture a picture. The others watched him in admiration for a moment then they took out their cans and began to spray too, but to Patrick they were just vandals. He, however, was an artist. So, it wasn't too bad what he was doing, was it?

But when he began to paint the figure falling, his hand froze, he felt his whole body go cold. He couldn't go on.

Cody stopped his spraying, watched him. 'What's the matter?'

Patrick took a deep breath. 'I'm an artist, Cody. Gotta get it right, you know?'

Cody laughed. So did Patrick. But he felt cold inside as he finished the picture, drew the man, his arms wide, sailing through the air, going down. He stepped back. It was good, yet he felt that something was missing. Something that should be there, and he couldn't quite remember what that something was.

'Fantastic!' Cody bowed in front of him. 'You're a master, Patrick. A master.'

The other boys howled their appreciation. Patrick felt good. Couldn't help it. Who else gave him compliments like this?

'Come on,' he said, taking charge for once. 'We better go. We'll get caught in a minute.'

Cody held him back. 'Just one more thing, the finishing touch.' Cody bent to the bottom of the wall, began spraying again. Patrick stiffened. He was going to spoil his work. Then Cody took a step back. He was laughing.

'There!' he said. 'Now it's perfect.'

And Patrick saw what he had added, and his blood ran cold.

TOO BAD IT WAS ONLY ONE

The other boys laughed. Patrick didn't. 'Bad idea, Cody. That'll cause trouble.'

That only made Cody laugh louder. 'Big deal, who cares?'

There was a sound at the other end of the underpass. Someone was coming. Patrick looked up. A huge black shadow seemed to fill the whole entrance. Cody pushed him. 'Time to go,' he said, and he began to run. Patrick took one last look at the painting, at the words written underneath. Yes, they were going to cause trouble.

And then he ran, following the other boys out back on to the estate.

Patrick had nightmares that night. His dreams were filled with them. Again and again, he saw that man falling, imagined his face, close against his own, as if Patrick too was falling alongside him in free fall. But they had no parachute.

'I don't want to die,' the man was saying. He reached out and grabbed at Patrick's hands, but he didn't want to die either and he pulled his hands away and the man was crying and screaming, 'Help me, please. Help me.' And he fell past Patrick, and instead of falling, Patrick rose like a bird, rose to the sky so he could see the very top of the tower block. He drew his eyes away from the falling man. So he missed, even in his nightmare, the sight of him hitting the ground.

8

'Did you hear about what was drawn on the under-pass?' Hakim asked Mosi as soon as he stepped through the school gates. Hakim was one of the other asylum seekers, an Iraqi, from Baghdad. A little older than Mosi, he was tough and hard and unafraid. He refused to step back from any fight. Mosi always kept well away from Hakim. Hakim asked again, his voice angrier. 'The underpass; did you hear what's been painted in it?'

Mosi had heard. He'd heard it muttered and whis-pered in the lift of the tower block, in snatches of conversation as he walked to school. 'I've heard,' he said.

'They're out to get us, Mosi. We have to stand up to them. We have to stand together.'

There were boys behind Hakim, watching for Mosi's reaction. Waiting for his answer. They despised him.

Mosi knew that. He didn't care. His answer was softly spoken, but firm. 'Better let it pass.'

Hakim's eyes flashed in anger. 'Let it pass?' He turned to his friends, no, not friends, they were for the most part, afraid to go against Hakim. 'Do you hear this dog?'

They all began muttering in anger, their fury aimed at Mosi. 'We're not going to let them walk over us,' one of the boys shouted.

Hakim pushed Mosi in the chest. He stumbled back. 'There was blood smeared all over that graffiti. I hope that was a message to whoever did it. A warning. Something bad will happen to them.'

Hakim looked over at Cody and his mates when he said that. Cody stared him down.

Then Hakim turned his attention back to Mosi. He pushed him again, and this time Mosi almost fell. He only just kept his balance. Still Mosi said nothing. Hakim spat on the ground. 'Coward!' he said. He beckoned his gang on with a nod of his head. 'Come on, leave him be. He's not worth the trouble.'

Mosi stood alone. He saw Cody and his mates sniggering at him. Bliss and her friends were watching him with something like pity in their eyes. He hoped she didn't come over. He wished all of them would just let him alone.

Patrick could feel the tension in the school. Everyone was talking about the graffiti in the underpass and the words written beneath it. He was sure they all knew it was him who had drawn that falling man, though any talent he had for drawing had never been noticed in school. Yet he was certain they were all watching him, whispering about him, waiting for him to scribble on a notepad, or scratch on a desk. He hoped no one would believe he could have written those awful words.

He should have stopped Cody doing that. In his mind he had. He had stood up to him, held him back from writing those words. If this had been a movie, that's what he would have done. But would it have made any difference? Or was the image he had drawn bad enough?

But the blood? They had had nothing to do with that. It had only made it worse. He remembered the figure in the underpass, that giant black shadow. Had he added the blood? And why would anyone do that?

'Blinkin' voodoo, that's what my dad says,' Cody insisted, and the others, apart from Patrick, all agreed with him.

It made Patrick sick to think of it. He'd never go out

and draw any graffiti again, he promised himself. He shivered, remembering his dreams, his night terrors. He'd hardly slept.

But a moment later, when Cody had looked across the playground at him, and winked, what had he done? He had winked back.

Bliss, of course, noticed it. 'What are you winking at him for?' She came right up to Patrick. 'You don't really want him for a mate, do you?'

'Maybe I just had something in my eye,' Patrick said coolly.

'You should keep back from him, Patrick,' she said.

'Wait a minute, are you actually going to say something bad about Cody?'

One thing about Bliss, she always found something good to say about everybody.

She shrugged. 'I just don't think him and you are a good mix. Did you hear about that graffiti?'

Did his face go red? He was sure it did.

Bliss was furious about that. 'That was terrible. How can people be that cruel? That poor man had a family.'

'Did he?'

'He had a brother, but he disappeared a couple of weeks ago, scared he was getting sent home. But he would have family back home . . . where was it he came from? Somalia, I think.'

Bliss would know. Her dad did a lot to help the asylum seekers on the estate. A lot of people didn't like him for that.

He hadn't thought of the man having a family, a brother, a mother. It made him feel even worse.

'Doesn't Mosi come from Somalia?' he said.

'It's a big country. He says he didn't know him.'

'Wouldn't admit it if he did,' Patrick said, his eyes watching Mosi, who was standing in a corner, alone.

'Anyway, I think whoever did it should be thoroughly ashamed of themselves.'

'I agree,' Patrick said, and he meant it, because he did feel ashamed.

'It's gone already anyway. The council had workers out this morning, cleaning it up.'

Gone already, but not before the television, the papers, photographers had their chance to capture the image for the evening news.

And by that evening, Patrick's handiwork was all over the TV.

And the blood.

9

There was a man and a woman in the flat when Mosi got home. Mosi recognised the woman. She'd been to the flat before. Rose Myer. She was from some group who were meant to help asylum seekers – but all she seemed to do was to tell them how miserable they should be; how grim the estate was; how little hope they had. She was the most miserable woman Mosi had ever met. And here she was again, dragging misery along with her like a suitcase on wheels.

The man he had never met, though he seemed familiar. He stood up when Mosi walked into the living room, and his tanned face broke into a grin.

'This is Grant Gray,' Rose Myer said. She was smiling now too. He'd seen her smile before, but it never lasted. As if the moment it landed on her face, it knew it didn't belong there.

Grant Gray. The name meant nothing to Mosi. But he definitely recognised the face from somewhere.

'Had a bad time in school today, Mosi?' Grant Gray asked, though it was more like a statement. And Mosi remembered now exactly who he was. One of those people who *wanted* things to be bad for them. It suited their agenda. Mosi had met many of them since he came here. He remembered too where he'd seen his face. He'd stood for the local council and his face had been plastered on posters all over the estate.

Grant Gray didn't wait for his answer. He sat down again. He turned to Rose Myer and his mother and father. 'I was afraid this would happen. The man who died was a Somalian, I knew they would take it out on all of you, the other African asylum seekers, target the children.' He looked again at Mosi, his blue eyes boring into his, as if his welfare was all he cared about. 'I need you to know that you don't have to put up with anything at school. Report everything that happens. We're setting up a daily club.' He nodded to Rose Myer. She was the other part of the 'we'. 'It's in the community room at the bottom of this court. You can come in there any time. If you have any problems, anything you want to talk about, just pop in. Someone will always be there.'

'This family keep themselves to themselves,' Rose Myer said, as if it was a fault. 'Isn't that right?'

His father spoke. 'We just don't want any trouble. We don't want to risk our chance of being allowed to stay.'

Grant Gray snapped the next words out. 'That's the problem. They want to make you victims.'

In Mosi's opinion it was the Grant Grays of this world who were the ones who wanted them to be victims. So he could fight for them.

'We've had no real problems,' his father said. 'People have been very kind.'

'They never say a bad word about anyone,' Rose Myer said, as if she didn't believe them.

'You don't have to be afraid,' Grant Gray said. 'We're here for you. The man who died thought there was no one there for him. We don't want you ever to think that. OK?'

'They mean to be kind,' his father said when they'd gone.

'They could make as much trouble for us as anyone else,' his mother said. 'I wish they would leave us be.'

Mosi lay on his bed that night, more worried than he'd been in an age. He could hear a police siren in the distance, hear the whoops of boys as they ran rampaging through the estate. The police would be here for a while, asking questions, looming round them.

Hakim, too, he was sure was going to cause trouble. He was aching for a fight. Him and Cody were already squaring up to each other.

And all because of the man who fell.

He only hoped he and his parents could stay out of it. It was all he wanted.

Patrick's mother had ranted about the police hanging around the flats. 'Asking questions. The way they're acting, you'd think we'd done something wrong. And they've only interviewed you the once. I think that's ridiculous. You're a key witness.'

His mother was contradicting herself, he could see that, but Patrick was glad it had only been once. He wanted to put it behind him, try to forget it.

Cody was raging about it too. He phoned Patrick that night. 'You'd think we were the ones that pushed that guy over the edge.'

But Patrick knew the tension had been raised by the graffiti he had drawn. That image, and the words Cody had written. And the blood . . . Who had smeared it with blood?

'I mean this is our country, our estate. They're the visitors here.' Cody had ranted on.

You're supposed to treat visitors with respect, Patrick wanted to say. Wished he had the nerve to say it to Cody.

'Are you coming out the night?' Cody asked him. And before he could answer Cody added, 'I think we better leave the graffiti for a while, eh?'

It was the best news Patrick had heard all day. 'Definitely,' he said. 'Anyway, I don't think I'll make it tonight.'

Cody sighed. 'Don't think I'll get oot either.' He tutted. 'If this keeps up, I'm gonny get really mad at somebody.'

10

Just as well he hadn't made any rash promises to Cody anyway, because there was no chance of Patrick getting out that night. His granny arrived. She walked into the living room after tea and hugged him. 'How are you, son?' she said.

Patrick couldn't speak. He was squashed against her. His granny was a big woman; she nearly smothered him. She pulled him down beside her on the couch. 'I wish I could have been here.'

'I was here,' his mum reminded her.

His granny glared at her. 'Not for long, I bet.'

His poor mum never knew how to answer his granny. She just shrugged. 'Patrick knows I'm always here for him.'

'Away and make us a wee cup of tea,' his granny ordered. 'And a sandwich for me,' she shouted when his mum was safely in the kitchen. 'That is, if you've got anything that's not past its sell-by date in that fridge.'

She hugged him again. 'A lot of bad things are happening on this estate. I don't like it.'

'It wasn't me,' Patrick said, out of habit.

She pinched his face. 'Of course it wasn't you. I just mean . . . that man throwing himself off the roof, and his brother disappearing, and all these weird things happening. That dead cat for one. That was awful.'

Patrick interrupted. 'Did you hear about the blood in the underpass?'

'Oh aye, I heard. That graffiti was shocking. Whoever did that wants to be locked up.'

At that point Patrick began to cough. Wished he hadn't mentioned the blood now. 'Do you think it's all connected, Granny? Do you think it might be voodoo? That's what people are saying.'

He didn't mention the 'people' were only Cody and his dad. Not that anyone would ever believe them.

'Naw, naw,' she said. She brushed that idea away as if it was an annoying fly. 'That's the kind of thing people say to cause trouble. There's a lot of gangs here on this estate. That's what it'll be. Always up to something.'

Patrick could hear his mother on her mobile in the

kitchen. Probably explaining she would be late going out tonight . . . if she ever managed to get out at all.

'You can't blame the asylum seekers for the weird things that have been going on. I could tell you a few stories about the strange things that went on when I was a wee lassie,' his granny said.

'I know, you told me.' His granny was always regaling him with stories from her childhood. 'I remember you telling me about them. Teddy boys,' Patrick said. He remembered her tales of funny looking guys who wore long pointed shoes and had weird haircuts.

'That's right. They ran about in gangs called The Tongs. Bad boys, some of them.'

He had heard all her stories. 'But nothing as weird as this, Granny,' Patrick said, with certainty.

She looked right at him. 'Oh, do you think your generation's cornered the market on weirdness?'

'Well.' Patrick hunched his shoulders. 'I mean, people disappearing, suicides, strange things happening round the estate . . . headless cats hanging in the underpass?' He said it in a 'beat that' kind of tone.

A wicked smile appeared on his granny's face. Then she said, quite casually, as if it was the most natural thing in the world. 'Well, we had a vampire.'

11

Patrick thought he'd heard her wrong. He almost fell off his seat. 'Did you say a vampire?'

'Oh, indeed I did. It's a well-known story,' she said. 'The Gorbals Vampire, they called it. There were things happening then as well. Weird things. Children had gone missing . . . two boys had been kidnapped, at least, that was the rumour.'

'Kidnapped!' Now she had all his attention.

'Och, that wasn't the worst of it. We heard they were eaten as well.'

'Eaten!' Patrick could hardly take this in. Eaten?

'Och, that's what they said anyway.' His granny went on. 'We didn't know if that was true. Didn't matter. We believed it. Then, out of the blue, we started hearing stories about a vampire roaming the Necropolis. That was what they call the big cemetery in Glasgow. City of the Dead. Well, once the rumour started that there was a vampire, it spread. Like Chinese whispers. The story went from one school to another. And got weirder with every telling. He was seven feet tall, with iron teeth. You could see his teeth shining in the dark, they said. The teachers tried to tell us it was nonsense . . . but I was nine. Who was I going to believe? A teacher, or my big brother? He was your age, and he was totally caught up in it. I believed it. We all believed it.'

Patrick was silent for a moment. 'Are you winding me up, Granny?'

'Not at all. We all got so worked up about it, and scared, that we decided to go out after school one night and watch for the vampire at the cemetery.'

'Did . . . did you see it? The vampire.' He waited for her to say no. He expected it.

'Well, do you know, I could have sworn I did. But see, that's what happens. When you're all caught up in some- thing, you can make yourself believe you saw anything. Some of the older boys, my brother included, they went into the cemetery. The rest of us sat on the wall, waiting. I seem to remember there was a full moon.' She hesi- tated. 'But that might just be my imagination. Anyway, we waited for ages . . . Next thing, there was all this

47

shouting and screaming, and the boys all came running out of the cemetery as if the Devil himself was after them. 'He's in there. He's there!'

His granny shouted it so loud, Patrick fell back.

'And I saw something moving in the cemetery. I was sure I did. Like a dark shadow. A giant shadow. We all saw it. And somebody screamed, 'That's the vampire!' And the place went crazy. There was a stampede. Weans were running everywhere. I fell off that wall, and skinned my legs. And I ran for home. I've never run so fast in my life.'

'Do you mean . . . you really saw a vampire?' Patrick was mesmerised.

His granny shrugged. 'At the time I didn't know what I saw. We certainly never heard about the vampire again. But we always said that it would come back, to have its revenge.'

The story sent a chill down Patrick's spine.

'How come you've never told me this story before, Granny?'

She hesitated. 'You know, I think I actually forgot all about it.'

'What made you remember?'

She was thoughtful for a moment. 'I think it's the

things that have been happening here. That was a terrible thing you saw, son, that man dying.' She hugged him closer. 'Maybe it's just a bad feeling. It made me remember how it all started with us. Way back then. One rumour led to another, it went from school to school, and it all got out of hand. It was a kind of mass hysteria.'

'Do you think the vampire's come back, Granny?'

'Well, if you see a seven-foot-tall man with iron teeth hanging about, let me know.' And then she laughed and punched him playfully. 'It was in our imagination, son. A great story to tell your grandchildren, but it wasn't true. There are no such things as vampires. But at that age you want to believe in them, don't you?' She let out a sigh. 'I'm telling you that story to let you know that there's always been strange things going on. Nothing to do with the asylum seekers and nothing to do with voodoo.'

Just then his mother came through from the kitchen with two mugs of tea in her hands. 'Oh, Mum, I wish you would stop telling my Patrick things like that. You'll give him nightmares.'

His granny let out a bellow of laughter. 'Me! You let him sit up half the night watching horror movies. I'm filling him in with a wee bit of Glasgow history. You're the one giving the boy nightmares!'

His mother never could win over his granny.

'I don't. I'm very careful what he watches on TV.'

'You're never in to see what he watches!'

They went on arguing back and forth, but Patrick wasn't listening. He felt as if a light bulb had been switched on above his head. He remembered that dark shadow in the underpass, the blood spread over the graffiti. And though he had never seen it, he could picture the headless cat hung in the underpass. It hadn't been any of the asylum seekers who had made all those terrible things happen. Nor any of the gangs. The thought was beginning to take hold that there might be another answer to everything that was going on here.

Perhaps the vampire was back.

12

There was a meeting in one of the community halls that night. Local councillors were coming, and representatives of the asylum seekers, the residents' association and the media. Journalists flocked in like vultures. The police were there too, just in case there was any trouble. The television cameras were practically camped on the estate, aware of the bubbling tension, ready to capture it on camera and eager for it to boil over.

Mosi wished they would all leave. They were only making things worse – their questions, their assumptions about who was to blame creating even more antagonism between the people here.

His parents didn't go to the meeting. Even though Grant Gray came to the door for them, willing to escort them, offering his protection so they could walk in safety to the hall in the next tower block.

'We do not need an escort,' his father said, more than once.

'But you really should be there,' Grant Gray kept saying. 'This meeting is to let people talk about what can be done to improve relations on this estate.'

'You don't live here,' his father said softly. Grant Gray, Mosi had heard, lived in a very nice detached house in the west end of Glasgow.

Grant Gray laughed. 'Yes, that's true, but I want to help. That's all I want.'

But he didn't, Mosi thought, as he listened from his bedroom. Grant Gray wanted someone to blame. He wanted confrontation.

He heard another voice break in. 'Why do you sit in fear in your home when the people need you? We must stand together on this.'

Mosi recognised the voice. It was Hakim's father. He was a spokesman for many of the asylum seekers, never afraid to speak out. Like his son. 'You're a coward.'

For a moment, there was silence. Then Grant Gray started to mutter. 'No, no, certainly not that. I know you fear your application for asylum will be turned down.'

Mosi heard the door closing on Grant Gray even as he spoke. 'Think what you wish of me,' his father was saying.

Mosi came out of his bedroom. 'If only they knew, *aabo*,' he said, 'just how brave you really are.'

His father smiled. 'Thank you, Mosi.'

Mosi was glad his parents had not gone to the meeting. There had indeed been trouble. Disruption by a group of residents who felt they were being unfairly blamed for the suicide. Blows had been struck, arrests made and, of course, the cameras caught it all.

And when Mosi went to school the next day, the atmosphere was even more tense.

Hakim almost leapt at him as he tried to get in the front entrance. His father, Mosi had heard, had been attacked at the meeting. He was angry about that. 'Here comes the coward!' he shouted. 'Your father's a coward. Your mother's a coward, and so are you.'

He thought by insulting Mosi's parents he would make him fight. But Mosi only tried to move past him. Hakim barred his way. He was much taller than Mosi. 'Is there nothing that would make you stand up for yourself!'

Again Mosi said nothing. Hakim pushed him. 'You should be ashamed.'

Mosi stepped away from him, still saying nothing. He

knew that it was only making Hakim more angry. He punched Mosi in the chest.

It was Bliss who came between them. 'See, you, Hakim, you're always picking fights.' She tugged at Mosi's sleeve. 'Come on, Mosi.'

'Yes, go with your girlfriend. You're safe now.' Hakim spat on the ground. 'But this isn't finished, Mosi. I'll see you later. That's a promise.'

'Don't listen to him, Mosi,' Bliss said softly. 'I think it's really cool the way you keep out of trouble. I don't think you're a coward.' She left him at the classroom door with a reassuring smile, then she went over to her friends.

But there was to be no peace for Mosi.

'Och, is that not nice? Bliss looked after you.' It was Cody and his friends making their way towards him down the corridor. Mosi took a deep breath. Cody looked angry too, as if Mosi had done something to him.

'Your lot caused a riot last night. Do you hear me? A riot! We're fed up wi' the whole lot of you.'

His mates gathered round Mosi. Cody sprang at him, grabbed him by the collar and pushed him against the wall. 'I want you to say it's all your fault. Right. Say it!'

Mosi hesitated for a moment. 'It's all your fault,' he said, his voice flat. Cody's eyes flamed.

'Ya wee . . .'

A voice came behind him.

'Leave him be. He's not one of us.' It was Hakim, and his friends rallied round him too. He nodded at Mosi. 'He could never be one of us. If you want a fight, Cody. Here we are.'

Cody threw Mosi aside. He was forgotten. He stepped towards Hakim, one boy as tall as the other. 'Any time, Hakim.'

13

With a wild howl, Hakim rushed towards Cody. Cody was ready for him, moving towards Hakim just as fast. They locked together like stags, and with equally wild howls the other boys jumped into the fight.

Patrick had just come into the corridor when it started. Glad he'd missed the beginning because he knew Cody would have expected him to back him up. Would he still expect him to jump in, join in the fight? Patrick stood still as a statue. Watching, because any second now teachers would come rushing down the corridor, alerted by the yells. They'd all be in deep trouble. For once, he wanted to keep well out of it. He saw Mosi turn his back and walk away. Everyone else was glued to the spot, could look at nothing else but the fight. But not Mosi. It was as if the fight wasn't even taking place.

How could he do that?

There was a sudden crash of doors bursting open throughout the corridors. Teachers appeared, running, shouting. The caretaker too was bounding towards them. Another teacher came rushing in through the entrance, sending the door bouncing back on its hinges. They were all heading towards the fighting boys. Patrick shuddered when he saw a punch meant for Hakim land on the teacher. Cody leapt back, his eyes wide. That was a punch too far. All of the boys fell back. Mr Gillespie grabbed Hakim by the collar. The headmaster was a big man, powerful, he almost lifted Hakim from the ground.

But Mr Gillespie didn't forget Cody either. With one quick movement he had Cody by the arm too.

'It was him started it,' Cody shouted.

Hakim began shouting in his own language. Hakim always fell back on his own language when things went wrong. Cody was shouting just as loudly.

'Shut up, both of you!' Mr Gillespie's voice thundered. He was lifting them almost off their feet, pulling them along towards his office. Still they both shouted and yelled, blaming each other.

Patrick felt good. He was glad he wasn't involved. It made such a pleasant change not to be included among the troublemakers. His eyes searched out Mosi. He stood as far away as possible from any trouble. Was he feeling the same way, he wondered. But Mosi was never in trouble. He made sure of it. Even though he was reviled by both sides, he didn't seem to care.

Mosi was a strange one. No doubt about that. He'd love to know what was going on in his head.

Mosi was thinking that if he could have made himself invisible he would have. There were people in his native land who believed it possible. That magic could be summoned and a man could disappear. If only he had that power. But he had no such power. He had no magic to make him invisible. So all he could do, all he had ever done, was to step back, and keep his head down. Make himself as invisible as humanly possible. He knew all sides hated him. He did not care.

He saw Patrick watching him. He too had kept out of trouble this time. Had he thought no one had noticed? But Mosi had seen him stepping into the corridor, seeing Hakim and Cody locked together. Patrick could have dropped his bag and joined in, could have leapt into the fight. But Patrick didn't. He had held back, and stepped away. Just as Mosi always did.

Bet he was glad he had, Mosi was thinking.

14

Mr Gillespie wasted no time in gathering the whole school together, his voice thundering round the assembly hall.

'I do not care what is going on outside the gates of this school, but in here, we will be a haven of peace, diplomacy and tolerance. There will be no fights. The parents of the boys involved in the fracas this morning will be informed of what has gone on here. But if there is one more . . .' His voice became a roar. 'One more bit of trouble, or bad feeling, fighting, or arguments, I will take this even further.'

'Take no prisoners, Gillespie,' Patrick whispered to anyone he thought would listen.

They were all blaming each other for the things that were going on here. The locals blamed the asylum seekers, and the asylum seekers thought the locals were the cause of it all. Things were only going to get worse and worse.

Patrick hadn't had a single moment to tell anybody about what his granny had told him and he was itching to talk about it.

Finally, he got his chance. He held Cody back as they walked into class after the assembly. 'Did your dad ever tell you about a Glasgow vampire?'

'A . . . what?'

Patrick said softly, 'A vampire . . . years ago, there was a vampire, right here in Glasgow. My granny told me.'

He decided not to tell him his granny didn't believe it any more.

Bliss had heard every word. She came towards them, her arm linked in Ameira's. 'My dad told me about that. It happened in 1954, the Gorbals Vampire they called it,' she said. And much to Patrick's annoyance, she started to tell Cody the whole story. Not half as well as he would have done. A crowd was gathering around them now. Most of them had never heard the story.

'Anyway,' Cody said. 'What has this got to do with anything?'

'Don't you see . . . the dead cat, the blood on the walls.' Patrick's eyes fell on Hakim listening intently at the back. 'Maybe it's the vampire. Back again. My granny says they all thought he would come back. For revenge.'

'Oh, come on, you don't really believe in all that stuff? My dad said it was just a rumour that got out of hand,' Bliss said.

'Yeah, but a lot of strange things have been happening here lately, Bliss,' Cody reminded her. Patrick could see the idea was beginning to intrigue him.

He didn't want to lose him now. 'My granny says it all started back then when two boys were kidnapped . . .' Naturally, Patrick didn't tell anyone that there had been no proof of that. 'And people have disappeared again. That man that died, Hassan, his brother went missing.'

'He ran away because he was being sent back . . .' Bliss insisted.

'Did he? Does anybody know that for sure? One minute he was here, and then he was gone.'

There was a long silence.

'That's the stupidest story I have ever heard.' Hakim pushed his way to the front.

Cody stood against him. 'Don't they have vampires in your country?'

'Of course we do, better vampires than you have. In our country, the vampires eat children.'

Cody laughed. 'You'd give them indigestion, Hakim.'

'And you would poison them.'

'But, that happened here as well,' my granny said. Patrick was bursting at the seams with the story. 'The two boys that were kidnapped,' he looked around. Made sure he had their complete attention before he added, 'They got eaten.'

15

By mid-morning, the story of the vampire had zoomed round the school. Whispers in the corridors, chattering groups in classrooms. Going from one to another, the stories growing more bizarre and gruesome with each telling. Some of the older pupils had heard about the vampire from their grandparents, but had forgotten it long ago. Now it came back and took hold. The blood, the hanged cat in the underpass, the missing man; maybe this was the explanation – a supernatural explanation. Not a human one at all.

Mosi heard the whispers but hardly listened. The whispers weren't shared with him anyway. He walked home, as he always did, alone. He could see a crowd of boys turning to watch him. He took another route, avoiding them. Mosi knew how to hide, ducking behind some buildings till it was safe to move on.

All the way home, Mosi kept close to the walls, an almost invisible figure. But not invisible enough. He had to come out into the open to cross the concourse to get into his own block.

And as he did, Hakim stepped from the shadows. 'Ah, there you are. I told you I would see you later,' he said. He had been waiting just for Mosi. Hakim moved in front of him. 'You make me ashamed.'

Mosi had no words to say to that. He knew even an apology would only anger Hakim more.

'You make us all ashamed.'

Out of the shadowy corners of the tower block, more of Hakim's gang appeared. They were all taller than Mosi. They seemed to fill the granite sky with their shadows.

Mosi took a deep breath. 'Please, let me pass.'

Hakim snorted a laugh. 'Please, let me pass.' He mimicked Mosi's voice. 'If you can get past us, you can go home, coward.'

He took a step closer to Mosi. Hakim had no intention of just letting him pass. Mosi had learned long ago that to run from trouble was a wiser option than to stay and fight. Especially when the odds were against you.

Mosi ran.

His sudden speed took them by surprise. He darted under one of the boy's arms, leapt away from a hand ready to grab him, and he was off.

'After him!' Hakim yelled.

Mosi raced across the concourse, through the abandoned children's park. He glanced behind him. They were all after him. He set the swings in motion as he passed, flinging one high, then another, their rusty squeak filling the silence, never once breaking his speed. He leapt the fence out of the playground and raced for the next tower block. He knew once he was round there, and out of their sight he could find a way back to his own block.

And then he saw Cody and his crowd hanging round the corner shop. He had to avoid them. One gang after him was enough.

Mosi thought of this estate as a jungle. It was a jungle for him, with danger behind every bush, in every clearing. He ran into the entrance of the next tower block. These blocks were all built to be the same, identical in every detail. He knew he could run past the lifts, up the stairs and find the back exit, and then run into the open again.

A couple of boys were sitting on the stairs, smoking. One of them tried to grab him as he ran past. 'What's the hurry, wee man?' The boy's voice was a growl. Mosi pulled away from his grip, kept on running.

He could hear the yells in the distance behind him. Hear the shouts. 'Where did he go? Where is he?'

Hakim wouldn't give up. He never had any intention of just letting him go home. Mosi running from him would only make him more determined to catch him. At the boarded-up convenience store, Mosi stopped for a second, pulling in deep breaths. He could hear the thunder of pounding feet coming closer. Cutting him off from the route back to his own flats.

He thought quickly. He would have to go further than he had ever gone. Mosi took the same route to school every day. The same road there, the same road back. A weekly visit with his mother to the shopping centre on the other side of the dual carriageway was the only deviation he ever made. He had no interest in exploring. But he had studied the estate from his tenth-floor window. He knew if he could sweep round the back of the estate and race through the underpass to the other side of the dual carriageway he could escape them. From there he would cross back again, go through the old cemetery and leap the wall into the estate. He would end up behind Hakim and the rest before they had even come out of the underpass. Mosi almost smiled at the thought of it. While Hakim and his gang were running on, searching for him, he would be heading for home. Mosi threw a glance behind him before he took off again. Let them come after me, he was thinking. I can run like a cheetah.

As he stood with Cody and the others, Patrick had caught a glimpse of Mosi in the distance. He had never seen anyone run so fast. A flash of a boy, gone in an instant. He almost pointed him out but stopped himself just in time. Cody hadn't seen Mosi. Too busy texting some of his friends about the vampire story. Patrick was glad of that. If he did see him, chances were that Cody would want to join in the chase. So Patrick said nothing. Mosi was only there for a second anyway, a blur of movement and then he disappeared silently into one of the other high-rises.

Then he saw Hakim and his friends, after Mosi.

He might have felt sorry for Mosi, wanted to help him. But why should he? Mosi had never done anything for him. Anyway, Mosi was safe. Running like that? He could easily get away from Hakim.

He didn't need any help.

At least, that's what Patrick thought.

16

Mosi kept running. He knew where he was going now. After he'd gone through the underpass, he could double back and head for home.

But why was Hakim always after him? Mosi was always alone, maybe that was why. Or perhaps because he would not join his gang. Yes, Mosi was easy to pick on. But not easy to catch.

Mosi leapt down a flight of steps leading to the path, slipped on some wet leaves. He took a moment to steady himself. He was sure Hakim would never think he would choose to go into the underpass. It was pitch-black in there. The lights were all broken. Lights never lasted in the underpass, the bulbs stoned minutes after they had been replaced. He took a breath, and began to run again.

He was only one step into the darkness of the under-pass when he saw the group of figures. They were huddled together. Mosi stopped dead. It was clear from the menacing way they were standing that something was happening here.

There were four of them, young men, but much older than Mosi. He could hear the threatening growl in their voices. There was another figure crouched against the wall, hands clutched around his head as if he was trying to protect it. Mosi saw the flash of steel. One of those boys had a knife, he was lifting it high.

In almost the same second, Mosi saw that it wasn't a knife at all. It was a machete. The boy was swinging it above his head. His ugly laugh echoed in the underpass.

Mosi couldn't help it, his first instinct was to run. Yet someone needed help. Someone was in danger. The boy holding the machete moved and Mosi saw his face and recognised him. Grady McManus, one of the worst troublemakers on the estate, who spent most of his time in custody.

Mosi could see a black shadow huddled against the wall, bent over, covering his head, the very image of fear.

Could Mosi help him? Mosi would never know, because in the same second that Grady dragged the man he was threatening into what little light there was, Mosi saw that man's face.

The man was looking up with huge eyes at McManus. And at the sight of that face and those eyes, Mosi was no longer among the grey tenements of Glasgow. He was back in his own land. He could almost feel the sun's heat against his face. Nothing else existed but the memory that came back to him like a scene from a film. He was watching this same man striding across the land, tall as a tree. He was in his uniform, medals glittering on his chest, sweat staining his shirt, a machete glinting in his hand. He crossed to a boy, a terrified boy, kneeling on the ground, his hands tied behind him. The boy was sobbing in terror. 'No, no, no . . . not me, not me,' he heard the boy cry. And Mosi had begun sobbing silently too. Trying not to watch, but Mosi was forced to watch, another man's hand forced his face up, so he was made to see. See what was to be done to that boy. 'I am Papa Blood,' the man in the uniform was saying, his voice cold as a grave. 'And this is what happens to those who disobey me.'

Mosi pressed himself against the wall of the underpass and bit against his knuckles. He pushed the memory away. He could not, would not remember that moment. It was too terrifying to remember.

And, now, this man, Papa Blood, was here. Crouching on the ground. Only a few steps from Mosi.

And at that moment he knew that it wasn't the man who was in danger. It was Grady McManus and his friends. It was all of them.

17

Hakim bounded into the underpass. He almost knocked Mosi off his feet. But Hakim looked beyond him. Took in what was happening, saw only an old man in danger.

'Leave him be!' he yelled. He pushed Mosi aside, began running towards Grady. That was the moment when the man cried out. Mosi heard his voice. Pleading for help. 'Help me, please . . .'

The voice sent a shard of ice down his spine. Because it was a voice he knew well, the voice of Papa Blood. Though he had never heard him plead before. Others had pleaded with him, and he had shown them no mercy.

Hakim's gang ran past Mosi; he was forgotten for the moment. Grady was outnumbered. Already his mates were running out of the underpass. Even with his machete Grady was not willing to stand alone. He threw the big man from him, began running backwards, shouting out to Hakim, taking in his face, remembering it. 'You're gonny be sorry for this,' he shouted, and then he and his mates were gone.

The man stumbled against the wall of the underpass. 'Thank you . . .' That voice was a murmur. In a moment he would recover. He would stand, he would look across at Mosi and . . .

No! Mosi moved back into the darkness as if he hoped the wall would swallow him up. What if he saw Mosi? Recognised him. He couldn't let that happen.

Hakim and his friends were helping the man to his feet. No time to lose.

Mosi began to run.

Patrick was on a swing in the park when Mosi ran into view. Cody and the others had all gone home.

'Hey, you're some runner, Mosi!'

Mosi ignored him. Patrick jumped from the swing. 'Hey, Mosi, is something wrong?'

Mosi was heading towards him, but he wasn't seeing him. His eyes had a wild look in them. 'Is Hakim still after you?'

He ran straight in front of Mosi, barring his way. And for a moment, Mosi stopped running. Patrick stared at him. There was something in his face that was scary. As if he'd seen something so terrifying he couldn't handle it. 'What is wrong, Mosi?'

Mosi didn't answer. He pushed him aside so roughly Patrick fell to the ground. Still he didn't stop. It was as if he hadn't seen Patrick at all, wasn't aware that Patrick was there. As if he was living in some other world, some other, terrifying world. Patrick called after him, 'Mosi!'

He wasn't even annoyed that Mosi ignored him. He could see so much terror in Mosi's face, in his eyes. Someone, or something, had scared Mosi half to death.

18

Mosi slammed into his flat, made straight for the bathroom and locked the door. His mother had called out when she heard his pounding feet. 'Is everything all right, Mosi?'

He took in a deep breath before he spoke. Wanted his voice to sound normal. 'Desperate to pee.' He heard her laugh. She laughed so rarely, and in that instant he knew he would not tell her who he had seen, nor would he tell his father. They knew of Papa Blood too, of course they knew of him, though they had never seen him. The memories of this terrible man were too raw for them. It would be his secret, at least till he found out more.

Why had he never seen this man before? Had he only just arrived here? Then, he hadn't seen Hassan, the man who died, and he had lived on this estate too. But he and his parents kept to themselves, didn't mix with others. Perhaps that was why he had never seen Papa Blood. How often had Mosi just missed him in the local shop, or almost passed by him on the pavement? And would he have recognised Mosi? Mosi began shaking again. No, his common sense told him, of course he wouldn't recognise Mosi. There had been too many boys like him.

Yet, in spite of the terror he felt, he slept all night. But his sleep was filled with bad dreams. Dreams that he was back again, with the jungle all around him. He was hiding in the bushes, and he could hear the feet coming closer and closer, hear the machete cutting through the thick undergrowth. Hear that man striding towards him.

The dream was so real that when he woke, shaking, he was sure he was covered not in cold sweat but in blood.

Hakim was quite the hero the next day. He stood in the playground telling anyone who would listen about his great rescue mission. And they were all listening, even Cody. He stood pretending he wasn't interested, but his head was bent to catch every word.

'A whole crowd of them were going to attack this old man,' Hakim was saying.

His friend Rami interrupted him. 'And one of them had a knife.'

'It was a machete. It was a machete!' Hakim quickly corrected him.

There was a gasp from the crowd.

Cody couldn't keep his mouth shut. 'You mean it was a big knife.'

Hakim glared at him. 'It was a huge machete. He was swinging it around like this.' He began swinging an imaginary weapon around him. 'Ready to attack this poor old man . . . and I saved him.'

Rami nudged him. Hakim glanced at him, looking annoyed, but he amended his story. 'Me and my friends, we saved him.'

'The old man was so grateful,' Rami said. 'He was so scared.'

'I hope you took him straight to the police.' This was Bliss, right at the front, her arm linked in Ameira's.

'No. We wanted to. But he refused. He doesn't want any trouble,' Hakim said. 'I can understand that.'

He said it as if he didn't understand it at all. Hakim would have loved the publicity, and he would have been even more of a hero.

'Did you know the old man?' Bliss asked.

Mosi tensed as he listened to the answer. Hakim shook his head. 'No, I didn't. But Mohammed did.' He turned to another of his friends. 'Didn't you?'

'It was Mr Okafor,' Mohammed said. 'I've seen him around.'

Okafor. The name meant nothing to Mosi.

Ameira let out a dramatic yell. 'Oh, I know Mr Okafor, he lives in the little houses next to my block. You know, the ones for the old people or the disabled. He's supposed to be really nice.'

Mosi shuddered as he listened.

Hakim's eyes flashed. 'He is a big man, but he walks bent over . . . like this.' Hakim began walking round the yard bent double. There was a flutter of girlish giggles. He straightened up. Tapped his brow. 'I think he's a bit soft in the head.'

Bliss nodded. 'Yes, something terrible happened to him. Isn't that what you heard, Ameira?'

Ameira's expression mirrored Bliss's. Her big brown eyes wide, her mouth open. Girls, Mosi thought, they were the same all over the world. 'He was attacked in his old country. He was left with permanent brain damage. But I've heard he is such a lovely man. Helps everybody. But keeps to himself. Very quiet.' She smiled up at Hakim. 'That was so brave of you to help him, Hakim.'

Hakim grinned back at her.

Mosi listened, and he thought, *Could that be true? Could this man be so brain damaged that he had changed . . . and in the same second he wondered, and did it matter?*

Cody stepped forward. 'The guy with the machete, Hakim, did you recognise him?' Cody answered the question himself. 'I know who it would be, he runs with a machete. Grady McManus.' He looked right at Hakim, for once not threatening or ready for a fight, but genuinely warning him. 'If that was Grady McManus, then you'd better watch out. He doesn't forget something like that. He'll be after you.'

19

Patrick stood at the back of the crowd, taking in Hakim's every word. He was sure he could never be that bold, to run in and save someone, and certainly not from a man with a machete. Especially if that man was Grady McManus. But he could picture the scene in the underpass as if he had been there. The steel blade rising, the old man bent and terrified, and Grady McManus. Patrick knew Grady, almost everyone did. Bad news – always had been. Cody was right. He wouldn't forget Hakim spoiling his fun.

Hakim's eyes caught sight of Mosi, standing away from the crowd. He stabbed a finger at him. 'This coward, he ran off and left him!'

They all turned to Mosi.

Hakim took a step towards him. 'He was in the underpass. He saw what was happening . . . and he ran off.'

'He was on his own, Hakim.' Bliss, as usual, sticking up for people. 'He couldn't do anything on his own.'

Hakim's eyes didn't leave Mosi. 'He could have stayed and helped us. Instead, he ran. The man's from his country, I bet. And he just left him.' He spat on the ground. 'Coward.'

Hakim began the story again as more joined the group eager to listen. Patrick kept watching Mosi.

Mosi's expression didn't change. There was neither guilt nor shame there. But why had he run so fast? Patrick had never seen anyone as scared as that in his life. The fear on his face hadn't been caused just by seeing an attack in the underpass.

Mosi had seen something different.

Something much worse.

Mosi passed him as he went into the school building. 'I saw you last night, Mosi,' Patrick said softly.

Mosi looked at him, and Patrick could see he didn't remember running past him. His mind had been filled with something else. Something so terrifying it had pushed everything else out.

Patrick's imagination went into overdrive. What would make him so scared? 'I know you saw something last night, Mosi. Something terrifying.'

Mosi flinched. His eyes grew wide. A reaction at last. 'I don't know what you mean . . . I saw nothing. Leave me alone.' Then he said the same thing in his own language. '*Idaa!*'

Patrick didn't know whether Mosi was lying, or if he honestly could not remember. Surely, no one could look so frightened and not remember what they had seen. It was bad not to remember. He'd seen a film once where the hero had a locked-in memory that had to be . . . well, unlocked. Mosi couldn't even remember seeing Patrick. Maybe everything else about last night was blocked out of his mind too.

Patrick was sure he had to be right. Mosi *had* seen something terrifying. There was only one way to find out. He was going to keep his eye on him from now on.

Patrick's words bothered Mosi all day. How could Patrick possibly know that he had seen something that scared him? Had he been somewhere, hidden in the underpass too? And even if Patrick had seen him, seen the man who had terrified him, he couldn't have recognised Papa Blood? There were no photographs of this most hunted of war criminals. That was why he had evaded capture for so long.

Mosi's mind swirled like water in a whirlpool. Papa Blood was calling himself Okafor. So this man, who had been a terrifying warlord back in his own country, was now known as Mr Okafor. He must be here under a false passport. Was he posing as an innocent asylum seeker, just like Mosi and his parents?

But people said he was soft in the head. His brain had been damaged. Had something happened to him? Had he been beaten, just as he had beaten others?

Had he been shot in the head, just as he had shot others?

He was a lovely man, Ameira had said. Everyone seemed to like him.

Had he changed so much?

Or ... and now Mosi faced another possibility. In fact, he wished for it. Prayed for it. As he had never prayed before. Was it possible he had been mistaken? There in the dark of the underpass how could he have possibly been so sure? The man he had seen was tall, with the same dark face, but how could he be so certain that this was the same man? Perhaps this man was really Mr Okafor – a man to be pitied, not feared.

And in that second he knew, though the thought terrified him, he knew he was going to go to where Okafor lived. He had to see him again, and find out the truth.

20

Patrick's granny had decided to camp out at his flat. She was there when he went home that day. Lying in wait for him as soon as he stepped from the lift. 'Where's your mother?' were her first words, as she held the front door wide.

Patrick shrugged and ducked under her arm. 'She must be at the bingo,' he said as he walked up the hall, slinging his school bag on the floor.

His granny closed the door and followed him inside. 'Is that daughter of mine never here when you come in from school?'

Never, he almost told her, but stopped himself just in time. It would only get his mother into trouble, and worse, in Patrick's opinion, it would keep his granny here for even longer. So he lied like an expert. 'Naw, she's always here, Granny. Nice tea ready for me and everything.'

'Ha!' Somehow, he was sure she knew he was lying. But it was worth a try. 'Have you got any homework?'

Patrick hesitated. 'Naw.'

She didn't believe that either. She threw his school bag at him. 'Right, well, let's get it done while we're waiting for your mother to come in.'

'I . . . eh, I had kinda plans the night. Meeting my mates and that.'

His granny pursed her lips. She looked as if she had just sucked a lemon. 'Not tonight, you're not. This is a school night. You are staying in.'

'But, Granny . . .'

'But Granny nothing! You're in for the night and that's final.'

How was he supposed to solve a mystery if his granny didn't let him out? He wanted to explain to her that he had to keep Mosi under surveillance. Mosi had seen something . . . something that had scared the life out of him. Patrick had to know what that something was. But he knew there was no way he was going to get past his granny tonight.

Mosi was even quieter than usual as he sat in his bedroom. His mother came in to see him. 'Has anything else happened?'

How could he tell her?

'There are many things going on.'

'We're not part of that, Mosi,' she said in her soft voice. 'Remember what we decided? We would keep our heads down, become invisible. Then we would be safe.'

Become invisible. The way to survive. Always the way to survive.

If only it was really possible.

He could become invisible. Papa Blood. Hadn't he told them that often? He could become invisible and soar like a great bird, soar above them, and see all. He was the breeze that brushed their cheeks. They could have no secrets from him. He was all powerful.

He could change his shape, become any creature he wished. He could slip into their minds so even their thoughts were not secret. Now, he was back.

It was too much. He would never escape from this man. Never. His mother left him, and he sat on his bed, rocking back and forth. He would never escape him.

Unless. Unless. He was not Papa Blood at all.

21

It was all Mosi thought about at school the next day. He paid no attention in lessons. He hardly listened. He would not go home. Instead, he would go to the block of flats where Ameira lived. He would find Okafor's house and he would see him in daylight. Then he would know.

He saw Patrick watching him all that day. He could see that he wanted to talk to him. So Mosi avoided him. He had nothing to say to Patrick.

As soon as the bell rang at the end of school, Mosi made sure he was out of the classroom and the school gates before anyone else. He slid behind the shop on the corner, where no one could see him. He watched Hakim take photos of himself and his friends with the new iPhone his uncle had given him for his birthday. He heard Cody and his crowd shouting and yelling as they ran down the road. There was Bliss and Ameira and some of the other girls, arms linked, giggling and chatting as they walked home. Finally, he spotted Patrick, last out. Probably thinking Mosi was still somewhere inside the school. He stood at the school gates, hands in the pockets of his hoodie, looking up and down the street. Mosi knew he was watching for him. He stood there for ages. Mosi thought he would never leave. It began to rain. Patrick pulled up the hood of his jacket, then with a puzzled look on his face he began to walk in the opposite direction, kicking at stones. Every so often he would glance around, and Mosi could almost read his mind. He was wondering how he had missed him.

Mosi waited in his hiding place till everyone had gone, till the road was quiet again. Then he too pulled up the hood of his jacket against the rain, trying to look invisible as he hurried towards the place where Okafor lived.

Patrick hadn't gone far. There was no sign of Mosi. How could he have lost him? But Mosi had been acting weird today. Shifty. Never making any eye contact. Moving away from him every time he tried to talk to him. Mosi was up to something. Patrick was sure of it. Something to do with what had scared him yesterday. Mosi definitely hadn't taken his usual route home, or Patrick would be able to see him somewhere on that long snake of a road. So where had he gone?

Halfway down, there was a path to the left that passed over the railway bridge and then wound round to the back entrance of the school. Perhaps he'd gone that way. Patrick took that path, and began to run.

He was out of breath when he stopped at the bridge. His eyes searched the pedestrian walkways and paths that led to the different parts of the estate. Where could he have gone? Yet, Mosi could hide. And he had seen how he could run.

What else could Mosi do, he wondered.

And just as he was thinking he might as well go home, Patrick saw him. He must have hidden somewhere outside the school and when it was safe, he had gone back in through the front gates and was heading across the playground, towards the back entrance.

It would have been easy to have missed him. His hood was up, and in that maroon hoodie he looked just like any other boy in the school. For that split of a second Mosi moved into the open. Then Mosi stopped, hesitated, looked back, as if he was unsure about whether to go on or turn back. But only for a second. Then he was gone again. Patrick didn't waste any time before he was after him. He wasn't going to lose him this time.

22

All the time he ran, Mosi was working out his plan. He would wait and watch for as long as he had to. He needed to see the man again. He had to be sure. He would make certain he wasn't seen, but even if he was, the man surely would not recognise or remember Mosi. He had only been one boy among so many, among thousands. But if he caught Mosi watching him, could he guess who Mosi was?

That thought stopped him for a second. Should he just go home? Forget he had ever seen him? Yet what choice did he have? He had to find out the truth. Mosi glanced back as he crossed the open playground. Once out of the back gates, he melted into the shadows.

The block where Ameira lived was the last on the estate. Behind it was a pathway, and then a high wall that blocked off the old cemetery that rose on the hill. Its dark grey headstones and stone angels seemed to loom in the background. For a moment the superstitious part of him believed it was a warning. Mosi stopped across from the entrance to the tower block. Beside it there was the long line of houses meant for the elderly or infirm with ramps leading up to the front doors. Ameira had said this was where he lived. Mosi stood inside the bike sheds. Though no one ever dared leave a bike here. Instead the sheds were filled with rubbish, and broken bottles and a couple of old prams. But he could hide here, out of sight. Hide here and wait.

It amazed Patrick how silently Mosi could run, how fast. He didn't even seem to make a sound as he splashed through puddles. How did he do that? Even running as fast as he could, Patrick almost lost him. But there, beside the bike sheds, he caught sight of Mosi's dark red hoodie, just as Mosi eased himself inside. Perhaps he was waiting for someone. Patrick slipped behind the bus stop. He saw how Mosi's eyes kept darting towards the houses. Or was he watching for someone coming out, or going in?

Ameira suddenly showed up. And who was with her? Big man Hakim, showing off, and waving round that blinking iPhone of his. Surely, Ameira couldn't fancy him! But it looked as if she did. It was all that talk of him saving Mr Okafor that had done it. Big show-off. They stood talking for a while. No, they didn't both talk. Hakim was doing all the talking, Ameira just seemed to be listening, hanging on his every word, giggling, it seemed, at all the right moments. Girls. Patrick would never understand them. And then, at last, with a little wave, Ameira went into her block, and Hakim left and darkness began to set in.

So why was Mosi here? Was he spying on Ameira? She was always nice to him and she was really pretty. It only took Patrick a second to dismiss that. Nah. This was bigger than girls. Much bigger.

How could Mosi stay still for so long? Patrick's legs were sore, his feet were cold. And yet, there was Mosi, still as death. Watching.

Patrick peered closer into the dark of the bike sheds. There was so little movement, he began to wonder if Mosi was actually still there. Maybe he'd slipped off home when Patrick had blinked, and he was just wasting his time.

And then, just when Patrick's resolve began to weaken, and in another few minutes he would have been off, he caught a movement. Mosi, standing erect, moving a couple of centimetres out of his cover. His whole body seemed to stiffen. His eyes were fixed on a point Patrick couldn't see. He looked puzzled. As if he couldn't figure out what he was looking at. Patrick tried to see but there was a stone pillar in his way. And then, the look on Mosi's face changed. Patrick had never seen a look of such terror. He was sure if he'd been closer he could have seen Mosi's whole body shaking. He tried to see what it was that Mosi was looking at, but it was blocked from his view. Mosi's gaze didn't shift. Patrick saw his hands grip his trousers, his fingers like claws digging deep into his skin.

What was he seeing?

Who was he seeing?

Patrick moved. He had to see what Mosi was seeing too.

23

In those first seconds Mosi was sure it wasn't him. Not Papa Blood. He'd been wrong, and he was so glad he'd been wrong. This man was bent over; his walk was more of a shuffle. He carried a bag of shopping. A child walked towards him and he reached out his shovel of a hand, a hand with a big cheap diamond ring on one of the fingers, and he patted her on the head. And then, he smiled. The smile of a gentle man.

The wrong man! Of course! How could he have mistaken this wreck of a man for Papa Blood? As if the most wanted war criminal in all the world could hide out here? In plain sight.

You're hiding out here, Mosi, a voice inside his head whispered.

But I'm not him.

I'm not evil like him.

Am I?

He wanted it so much to be the wrong man.

But what a disguise that would be.

He had to be sure. He moved a step closer.

Mr Okafor shuffled towards one of the houses. It had a ramp leading to the front door. It seemed to tire him as he walked, as if even that small climb was an effort. At the front door, he laid down his shopping bag, searched in his pocket for his key. He glanced around. There was no one about. The path around the tower block and the houses were deserted. And for a split second, he stood straight. Out of sight of the world, he straightened. Holding his back as if it pained him to have to stoop in such an unnatural position for so long, every day. Mosi held his breath, because in the same moment the man turned as if he knew someone was watching him. He looked all around, his eyes searching in every direction. And somehow, Mosi found the courage to keep looking, and he saw in that second the real man emerge, the stoop gone, the face with nothing of a smile left in it.

It was the face he remembered.

The face that haunted every one of his nightmares.

Once again he was where he did not want to be. He could feel the midday sun burning his back. Papa Blood was striding towards them. He held his machete in one hand, his gun in the other. Mosi made himself invisible. The only way to stay safe. He melted behind the boy in front of him, kept his eyes fixed on the ground. He had seen other boys try to please him, and he had seen his awful wrath turn against them when they displeased him. Or disobeyed his rules.

Better if he never saw you at all. Like now. Mosi shrank back, lowered his head. The man was angry. He had come for one of them. It didn't matter to him which one.

He stopped in front of the kneeling boys. Looked down at them. And when he spoke his voice was the voice of ice-cold terror.

'You have no one else but me to look after you now. You have no mama, no papa. I am your papa. I will look after you, take care of you. And if you cross me, I will punish you. I am Papa Blood.'

Some things you cannot bear to remember. That moment was one of them. Mosi's body began to shake, and no matter how he tried his mind flashed with horrific images, glints of steel, blood, people screaming, dying. He felt his legs go weak. He stumbled back into the bike shed and forced himself not to vomit. The monster might hear him. When he glanced back to the entrance to the house, the man was gone.

It was only Mr Okafor, Patrick was thinking, when he saw him standing at his front door. He had never seen him but, from Ameira's description, the bent back, the daft look on his face, it was definitely Mr Okafor. He was carrying a blue plastic bag. There was a carton of milk in there, and some bananas. He'd been shopping. Why was Mosi so terrified of this man? Hadn't Ameira said everyone liked him?

Okafor laid down his shopping bag, searched in his pocket for his front-door key. He looked around him, and then, he stretched up. The height of him made Patrick gasp. He had never seen anyone so tall. And for a moment, the daft look on his face seemed to disappear. He looked completely different. But only for a second. Then he opened his door, bent down to pick up his bag, and shuffled inside his house.

Patrick was puzzled. Mosi was terrified of Mr Okafor? Here was another mystery. And Patrick knew then, he would have to find out why.

24

Mosi had wanted to get far away from this man for so long. Yet, here he was on his estate. One day, he might come face to face with him. In a shop, in the street on the way to school. And he would give himself away, he knew he would. He would not be able to hide the horror in his eyes.

And what could he do? Where could he go? Nowhere was far enough to escape his magic.

He began to run. His legs wobbled under him. Before he reached the walkway, he was sick, and this time he didn't stop himself. He vomited so much he was sure there was no stomach left inside him.

He was still bent double when he felt the hand on his shoulder. He leapt with fear.

'Are you OK, Mosi?'

It was Patrick. Mosi wiped his mouth clean with his

sleeve. He didn't know what to say to him. What was Patrick doing here?

'I know, Mosi, I know who you're afraid of.'

Mosi still said nothing. He couldn't take this in. His eyes moved swiftly to the line of houses, almost as if they could see that giant of a man filling the rooms in his house with his presence, standing tall now he was alone again.

Patrick followed his gaze. 'I know he lives there.' He touched Mosi's arm. 'And you're terrified of him.'

Mosi pulled away from him, shaking his head. Patrick knew? How much did he know?

'I only want to help you, Mosi.'

'There's nothing we can do, Patrick. Nothing.' His words were a mumble. 'The monster is here, and there is nothing we can do.'

And he began to run home.

A monster? But how could that daft old man be a monster? What did Mosi mean?

Patrick tried to race after him, but in the seconds it took for him to absorb what Mosi had said he was gone. As if he had vanished. Not even the sound of his footsteps echoing on the concrete. It was too eerie. Patrick stopped dead. It was growing darker. He was alone on the pathway. With all this talk of a monster, and a vampire, Patrick imagined strange things all around him. The tower blocks seemed to close over him. The estate became a place Patrick didn't recognise. And when a dog howled somewhere behind him, Patrick was off too. Every moment he glanced around, sure something was after him. A shadow on the wall made him stumble, almost fall. But he managed to keep going. It reminded him of the giant shadow he had seen in the underpass. He felt as if round every corner that same giant shadow would leap out at him. He would be the next victim.

As he stepped into the lift he couldn't stop shaking.

Perhaps something was waiting for him in here, crouching on top of the roof, and when the lift began to rise it would leap through the hatch and be on him. He was even glad when the old man from the fifteenth floor ran for the doors and held them open. Old Mr Ratho, a wee bit drunk, a wee bit annoying, but the best company Patrick could have asked for. He talked non-stop as the lift rose floor by floor, and Patrick was glad he was there. He stood in the middle of the lift, swaying, right beneath the hatch. If something did drop down, it would get him first.

'Are you feeling OK, Patrick?' Mr Ratho asked when the lift reached his floor and Patrick stepped out. 'You're never usually this quiet. Usually cannae get you to shut up.'

Patrick licked his lips. 'Think I ate something,' he said.

The flat was empty. No Mum. No Granny. And for once he wanted one of them to be there. He put on all the lights and curled up on his bed, hugging his knees, listening to every sound.

25

Patrick was desperate to speak to Mosi the next day. He stood on the ground floor waiting for Mosi to come down in the lift. Waited so long he was late again for school. Yet, when he finally tore into the classroom, getting bawled at for being 'tardy again' – Mrs Duncan the English teacher was always talking like that. Trying to teach them new words, when half the class couldn't speak English at all. Mosi was there. Deliberately not looking at him. How had Patrick missed him? Even if he'd run down the stairs, Patrick would have seen him, going out through the main doors, running across the concourse.

Maybe he had a parachute.

Patrick sat three rows behind him and didn't take his eyes from the back of Mosi's head all through the lesson. Willing him to look round. But Mosi kept his gaze fixed firmly in front of him, as if he was engrossed by what the teacher was saying.

Patrick grabbed Mosi as soon as the lesson ended and the class were flooding to the next lesson. 'Mosi, we've got to talk.'

'Talk? About what?'

Patrick felt his face go red. 'About what? About yesterday, of course! About who you saw. About what you said.'

Mosi shrugged his arm free. 'I saw nothing. I don't know what you're talking about.'

Patrick wasn't going to let him deny it all. He spoke so loudly some of the others turned to look. 'Who are you trying to kid? I followed you. I know what you saw. Who you saw.'

Mosi backed away, shaking his head. '*Idaa!*' he said. 'Leave me alone.' But Patrick could see the fear in his eyes. Then, Mosi turned and ran.

Patrick stood watching him. Why was Mosi lying? Was he really that afraid? Yep, that was it. He was afraid, and Patrick couldn't blame him. He was afraid too. And he didn't even know what he was afraid of. But why lie?

Mosi was hiding something, terrified of something. Terrified of Mr Okafor. It didn't take a Sherlock Holmes to know that. But who was Mr Okafor? A monster, he had called him. Patrick couldn't leave it at that. He had to know more. All Patrick wanted to do was help. Couldn't Mosi see that?

'What was all that about?' It was Bliss, and beside her, clinging on to her arm, Ameira.

'I hope you weren't picking on Mosi.' This was Ameira.

That made Patrick laugh. 'Me? I don't pick on anybody. You should talk to your boyfriend. He's the one who picks on Mosi.'

A blush rose in Ameira's face. 'Me? I don't have a boyfriend.'

Patrick shrugged. 'If Hakim was my boyfriend, I'd keep it a secret as well.'

This time her face went bright red. 'He is not . . .' She couldn't finish what she was saying. Couldn't find the words she needed.

Bliss rescued her. 'So since when has Mosi been your best friend?'

'I was trying to talk to him about something important, if you must know.'

For a moment he wondered if he could confide in Bliss. She was really annoying at times, but she was a nice girl. She would want to help Mosi too. But Mosi was so scared and didn't want anyone to know about it. Maybe he should just keep his mouth shut for now.

'It was boy talk, actually.' He said it as if she had asked.

Bliss turned to Ameria. 'Boy talk! Must be something really boring, then.' And confident that together they had at least protected Mosi, they both walked off.

Mosi was glad he had had time to think about what to say to Patrick. He'd needed that time. Patrick had followed him, had seen his fear of Okafor. And for a while, just a short while, he'd been glad. Here was someone he could confide in. Together, they could decide what to do.

But what if Patrick wanted to know how he knew of this awful man? Knew he wasn't who he said he was. That he must be here under a false passport. How could he explain that he knew one of the world's most wanted war criminals? The truth would lead to all his lies tumbling like dominoes, one after another. And Patrick would want to go to the police, and Mosi's story would come out, and . . .

NO!

He could not confide in Patrick. If Patrick knew who Okafor really was, then let him go to the police on his own. He would say nothing. Pretend he had seen nothing. What was it Patrick had seen anyway? Mosi watching Okafor. Mosi being sick. He had put two and two together and come up with the wrong answer. Better to pretend he didn't understand what Patrick was talking about. And that would be the lie he would stick with.

Another lie.

And anyway, perhaps the man had changed. His past he could not change. He had been a monster, worse than a monster, nothing could make up for the past. But perhaps he was trying to build a new life here, just as Mosi was. As his parents were. Perhaps he was trying to make up for all the evil he had done.

Everyone deserved a second chance. Didn't they?

He would not let fear ruin things for him. He was going to forget Papa Blood existed. He would avoid ever being near him. Let Patrick do what he wanted.

It was in the afternoon that the whispered rumours started flying around the school. One wilder than the next.

It began with a body found in the cemetery.

But the story blazed out of control.

Cut into little pieces.

Blood everywhere.

Beyond recognition.

The police were back on the estate in force. Sitting in the classroom, everyone could hear the sirens.

A body found.

Let it be Papa Blood, Mosi thought. Then he could live without fear of ever seeing him again.

But that wasn't the whispered rumour that raced round the school and was sent on text messages from one school to another. For them, there was a growing excited suspicion.

The vampire had struck again.

26

Mosi's father was at the school gates waiting for him when school ended. Many of the parents were there. Mothers, fathers, carers. Mosi even saw Patrick's granny, a big broad woman with her blonde tipped hair cut in a fashionable bob.

'Why did you come?' Mosi asked his father.

His father put his hand on his shoulder. 'Have you heard about the body?'

Mosi nodded. 'We all did. I hoped it was only a rumour.'

'No rumour. Someone has been murdered.'

'Who . . . who was it?' Mosi was afraid to ask, afraid of the answer.

'No one knows yet. It doesn't matter. If it is one of the locals, we will all get the blame for it. If it is one of the asylum seekers, we will still have trouble.' His father looked worried.

As they walked home together Mosi could feel the tension on the estate. The police cars were there, cruising the area, watching for any unrest. There were groups of men standing talking; they ignored Mosi and his father, but their suspicious eyes followed them as they passed.

Patrick couldn't believe his eyes when he saw his granny at the school gates.

'What are you doing here?' He was looking around to see who else noticed her. But how could anybody miss his granny? For a start, she'd just had her hair done. She had blonde highlights and everything. Hair that looked totally out of place on his granny's head.

'I'm here because your mother isn't,' she snapped. At the same time she grabbed his shoulder and pulled him on. 'Have you heard what happened?'

'A dead body . . . I heard there was blood everywhere.'

'Oh, and you'll be adding to that, telling people there was a disembodied head rolling out of the cemetery, eyes popping out the sockets, I suppose.'

'Was there?'

She never answered him. Proof enough it was true.

'The body really was found in the cemetery?'

'There's already been trouble. A fight broke out . . . mind you, it was in a pub and they were all drunk, but it's a sign of things to come. So, we are in for the night.'

'What do you mean . . . we?'

'I'm staying at your place the night.'

The thought horrified him. 'But I've got to go out. I've got people to meet,' he said.

His granny stopped walking. 'You talk as if you're a blinkin' business executive. You've "got people to meet"! Well, call them up on your mobile and cancel your meeting.'

There was no chance of escaping from his granny's clutches. He was staying in whether he liked it or not . . . and he didn't like it. It was so annoying. Because this was one night he wanted to go out. Needed to. There was an excitement in the air. Patrick could feel it. He wanted to be part of it. But he'd never get away from his granny.

'Do you think that vampire might have come back, Granny? It's all they're talking about at school.'

She flicked her fingers against his head. Honest, between his granny and his mother, it was a miracle he wasn't brain damaged. 'That was only a story, Patrick. I believed it then. I was nine. We were all caught up in it. But I would never believe it now. Vampires don't exist. And let me tell you, son. Real life is a lot scarier than any vampire story.'

27

By morning, the identity of the dead man was known.

Mosi heard it as soon as he got into the school. Hakim and Cody, for once standing together, were clearly talking about it. Hakim called out to him, 'Have you heard who it was?'

Mosi shook his head. He held his breath, waiting for the answer.

It was Hakim who shouted the answer, pushing through his friends till he was standing in front of Mosi.

'It was Grady McManus.'

Mosi felt himself go weak. Grady McManus. Mosi could see him again in the underpass, his machete raised high, ready to attack Papa Blood.

Now Grady was dead.

'Remember him?'

'I remember him.'

'The night you left poor Mr Okafor to be chopped to pieces.' Hakim stepped closer. Too close. He lowered his voice. 'I don't trust you, Mosi, but I am warning you about this. We've all decided.' He waved his arms taking in not only his own friends, but Cody's too. 'We've all talked about it, and we've decided that we don't mention the old man. Or what we saw in the underpass. That never happened. He's a nice old man, everyone says so. Even Cody thinks it would be unfair to link him with McManus.'

Cody came across then. 'McManus had loads of enemies. There'll be a queue of suspects as long as your arm. We're not going to get that old guy into trouble.'

There was a murmur of agreement.

Hakim turned to Cody. 'You know, that old man wouldn't bring any charges against McManus. He just wanted it forgotten. So . . .' He turned his cold eyes on Mosi, as if he was the enemy. 'It never happened.'

Mosi only nodded his head.

'If that old man is questioned by the police . . . I will blame you.'

He threatened him because he could. He thought Mosi a coward, who would say nothing back to him.

Mosi said nothing back to him.

They drifted away from him, still talking. Grady's death seemed to have drawn them together. Mosi stood alone, his mind in a whirl. McManus had attacked Okafor. And now McManus was dead.

Papa Blood hadn't changed. He was the same monster he had always been. He had come after McManus, Mosi had no doubt of it.

But what could he do about it?

28

There was a fire on the estate that night. Mosi watched it from his bedroom window. Long tongues of flame reaching into the dark sky. Sparks of light rising like fireflies into the night. He could hear the sirens as they roared towards the blaze. His mother came into the room to watch with him. She placed a hand on his shoulder. 'It's on the other end of the estate. Far from us.'

'I wonder who started it.'

'Everyone hated this man, everyone was afraid of him. Yet, now he has become a victim.'

Mosi wondered what was on fire. It wasn't one of the tower blocks. It looked more like one of the boarded-up shops.

If the asylum seekers were now in danger because of Grady McManus's death, then it would all be Papa

Blood's fault. He had brought this on them. Mosi had no doubt about Papa Blood's guilt.

And his guilt too.

This would never have happened if he had told the authorities who Mr Okafor really was. He would have been arrested. McManus would still be alive. Papa Blood would have been gone from here.

But what if he had found out it was Mosi who had exposed him? And he could find out anything. The man had magic in him. He would know, hadn't he always known? He would find Mosi. He would come back for him.

Yet he had to tell someone, but who? And how could he tell and keep himself and his parents safe?

There was no way out of this. None that he could see.

Mosi wasn't the only one who felt guilty. Three floors up, Patrick was also watching the fire from his balcony. He was so dying to get out there, to get closer. But of course, his granny wouldn't let him out of the door. He felt sorry for his mother too. She'd been grounded as well. His granny had his mother slaving over a hot iron, getting his uniform ready for the next day. Meanwhile, she was in the kitchen, clearing out the cupboards, chucking out mouldy bread, and milk that had passed its sell-by date.

One thing about his granny, when she was here she got things done.

He looked across at his mum. 'She's driving me potty, Patrick,' she mouthed to him.

He nodded his agreement. They were definitely going to have to come up with a plan to get rid of her.

Then Patrick turned back to the balcony. He watched the flames rise to the sky. And even though his common sense told him how crazy it was, he could not get the picture of the vampire, lurking somewhere in the shadows, out of his head.

Mosi's mother walked with him to school next morning. He noticed that hardly any of the pupils walked alone.

There was still the smell of burning in the air. More fires had sprung up as the night progressed.

At the school gates, Patrick and his granny approached them. Patrick's granny was gripping him as if he was under arrest. She smiled at Mosi's mother. 'Would you mind if I walked back with you, dear? We live in the same block, don't we?'

119

She turned to Patrick. 'Away you go. I'll see you at finishing time.'

Patrick's face turned the same colour as his hair. 'I can walk home on my own.' He grabbed at Mosi's arm. 'Me and Mosi'll walk home together.'

Patrick's granny hesitated.

Patrick was determined. 'Aw, Granny, we'll be fine. There'll be a whole gang of us.'

His granny laughed. 'I'll think about it.' Then she smiled at Mosi's mother. 'You worry about them that much, don't you, hen. But don't worry. This'll all pass. That Grady guy had that many enemies they'll be able to fill two buses with the suspects.' And when she laughed, Mosi saw the beginnings of a smile on his mother's face too.

'Your granny is really kind,' Mosi said to Patrick as they watched them walk away. He saw that his mother was being chaperoned, protected, in a quiet way by Patrick's granny.

Patrick blew out his cheeks. 'You like her? You can have her. For nothing.' Then he pulled Mosi into a corner. 'Mosi, I've been thinking about this all night. I know you're scared of Mr Okafor. I saw how scared you were. You've got to tell me why.'

Mosi stepped back from him. He so much wanted someone to confide in, someone who might understand. Patrick had seen his fear of Papa Blood. He would not let this go until he knew at least a little bit of the truth.

'After school, Patrick. We will talk after school.'

29

Mrs Telford stood in front of them in class during registration, her face set like stone. The room was silent. 'There have been a lot of things going on in the area,' she began. 'These things have nothing to do with you. You did not cause them. And I want you all to know . . .' She paused, and her eyes passed round the classroom, taking them all in, one by one, 'and I mean *all* of you, that here, in this school, you have a place where you will be safe. There will be no tension here. No fighting. No discrimination. Here, we are all the same. If there is anything worrying you, come to me. Talk to me, talk to your teachers. We are all here for you.'

She meant it, Mosi thought as he listened. She meant every word. Yet when her eyes paused at his face, he was sure she meant her words for him alone. She knew his secret. And he could tell her about Papa Blood, and it would be all right.

If only.

Mrs Telford could try to make sure there was no tension in the school, but she couldn't stop the rumours, the whispers, about the fires, about Grady's death, whispers that grew more sinister with every telling.

There was a serial killer on the estate.

Grady's heart had been torn out.

It was voodoo.

But the whisper that grew louder as it passed was the same one. That it was the vampire, back again. That rumour seemed to grow with every passing moment.

Cody helped it along. 'My granda was there the last time it came. He went to the cemetery. He says he saw the vampire. Actually saw it.'

Patrick didn't believe a word of that. Cody was worse than Patrick for telling stories.

'This is just how it started before, my granda says. People dying in weird ways, or going missing.' Cody held up his phone at break time. 'I've just had a text from my mate at Park Green School. He says Grady's body was drained of blood. They think it was the vampire as well.'

Murmurs of horrified agreement.

'Everyone said the vampire would come back,' Patrick said. Caught up in it too.

Even Bliss began to be convinced, despite her common sense. 'My dad says there are no such things as vampires.' But she was trying to make herself believe that.

The weather too seemed to add to the mood. A leaden sky, and rain dripping from the railings. A mist hovering above the roof of the school. The day growing dark again before it had a chance to be light.

Murmurs of vampires wound through the school all day. It was all they seemed to talk about.

30

Patrick was waiting for Mosi when the school day ended. Mosi had almost hoped he had forgotten. His eyes darted round, looking for his mother. Patrick held out his phone. 'Called my granny, told her you and I were walking home together, there would be a whole crowd of us.'

'Do you always lie to your granny?'

Patrick shrugged. 'One of them white ones.'

Mosi fell in beside him. No choice. 'Where are we going?'

'Somewhere we can talk and not get disturbed.'

'Is there such a place?'

Patrick laughed. 'You bet there is, and I've found it.'

Buildings still smouldered. 'Look at that,' Patrick tutted his disapproval. 'Pure vandalism.'

He began walking backwards, talking to Mosi as he went. 'Have you been listening to the rumours, Mosi?'

Mosi didn't answer him. He had been too caught up in his own thoughts to care what others were saying. They came to an old deserted garage with a broken door.

'In here, come on. Nobody'll see us talking in here.' Patrick pulled a steel panel open, and squeezed inside. Patrick lowered his voice. 'He's been here before, you know.'

Mosi's head began to swim. What was Patrick talking about?

Patrick closed his eyes in a look of exasperation. 'The vampire . . . the whole school's been talking about it.'

Mosi shook his head. 'I didn't listen.'

'You're always in your own wee world, aren't you, Mosi?' He paused, waiting for Mosi to say something. But Mosi stayed silent. 'Why are you so scared of Mr Okafor? Who is he? You called him a monster. Tell me the truth, Mosi.'

How much could he tell Patrick? Where would he begin?

But there was no time for Mosi to think how to answer. There were footsteps behind them. Both boys turned at the sound. A group of boys were pushing their way through the broken door, one by one, sending their long shadows along the floor. Mosi recognised Cody, almost

126

the last to come through. The other boys were older and in an instant Mosi knew who they were. The other boys who had been in the underpass that night. Grady McManus's gang.

'Hey, Cody, what's this?' Patrick called out. His voice was full of bravado, but it shook just a little.

The old garage seemed to grow even darker. Mosi looked around for an escape. There was only one exit, that broken door, and those boys were blocking it.

Patrick hoped his voice didn't shake when he called out. He recognised Cody, and Cody's brother, JD. He'd only seen the others around the estate. Rough and hard. Friends of Grady's. And that was what made Patrick afraid. Afraid for himself, but afraid for Mosi too.

He shouted to Cody's brother. He wanted them all to know he knew them. 'Hey, JD, how's it going?' JD was usually a laugh. He wasn't laughing now. None of them were. Even Cody looked scared.

JD called back to him, 'Get out of the way, Patrick.'

The boy at the front suddenly produced a machete. Patrick felt his skin crawl. Now he saw what they intended. They were out for Mosi. He began to sweat. 'I didn't know they'd come after us.' He said it softly, to

Mosi, didn't want him to think he had led him here, that he'd lured him into an ambush.

Mosi's voice was soft. 'I know you didn't, Patrick.'

Patrick took a step closer to Mosi. To let him know he was on his side. 'Leave him be,' he shouted now and he didn't care if his voice did shake, because even Cody was shaking, as if this had gone further than he had expected or wanted. 'He's on his own. He's never done anybody any harm.'

Mosi was saying nothing. He looked tense. Patrick shouted now. 'JD, tell them not to touch him. Just let us go.'

But JD rushed at Patrick, took him completely by surprise. He grabbed him like a rag doll and threw him aside. Patrick landed against the wall and crumpled to the ground. He saw one of his best drawings on this wall. He remembered the night he'd done it, with Cody, remembered them laughing as they sprayed the paint on the walls. He didn't want it spattered now with blood. Mosi's blood, or his.

The boys were all circling around Mosi. He didn't stand a chance . . .

31

There was hate on their faces, so much viciousness. Mosi watched the machete, its long curved blade, its edge honed sharp. The boy waved it around. It gave the others courage. One of them giggled nervously.

'Look at the wee guy,' the boy with the machete said. 'Nearly wetting himself.'

'My wee brother said he was a coward. Even his own kind hate him,' another boy said.

This must be Cody's brother. Mosi could see him jumping from one foot to the other. Though his words were harsh, his voice trembled. He looked scared.

Mosi's eyes darted round for an escape route. He imagined himself ducking under their arms, leaping over their heads, darting one way, then another, till he was behind them. And then he would run like the wind and they would never catch him because no one could run as fast as he could. All these thoughts whirled through his mind like a tornado.

He had to get away, because he couldn't fight them. He wouldn't fight them.

But they were blocking the only escape route from this old garage. Mosi stepped back, and felt the wall behind him. He could go no further.

The boy with the machete drew in a deep breath. His voice was a snarl. 'It was your kind that killed Grady. With your voodoo.'

Patrick shouted out. His voice shaking. 'No . . . it wasn't him. Leave him!'

They weren't listening. Mosi recognised what was happening. He had seen it often before. Once the blood-lust was up, nothing could stop them from what they planned to do.

'Come on, let's get him.' Mosi didn't even know which one said it.

And they moved in.

This couldn't be happening. Patrick's legs were like jelly. He lost sight of Mosi as the pack closed in on him. Cody stood beside him; he was trembling. 'We've got to do something, Cody.'

But Cody was almost close to tears. He couldn't handle it. He shook his head, put his hands over his ears to blot out the sounds, and then he was running, out of the garage.

Patrick wanted to cry too. Mosi was darting one way, then another. The boys were laughing. In a moment they would strike.

He couldn't let this happen, but what could he do? He was only one boy. And then, it was as if some primal instinct took over. He didn't even know *what* he was doing. He began to yell, like some ancient Celtic warrior. He was roaring, 'Leave him be!' And he began to run.

He leapt on the boy with the machete. He jumped on his back just as the blade was lifted again. The boy yelled, 'Get him off me!' He tried to shake him off, but Patrick wasn't letting go.

The others grabbed at Patrick. He kicked out at them, sent one of them stumbling back and knocking into another. One of them grabbed at his hair and pulled. The boy with the machete twisted, reached back for him, tried to grab for him with his free hand, but Patrick dug his fingers into the boy's eyes. He let out a yell, but still he could not topple Patrick. But Patrick knew he couldn't keep this up for much longer. He shouted, 'Run, Mosi! Run!'

131

Mosi began to move, leaping behind the boys. The boy with the machete was swearing. He reached back again and grabbed Patrick by the hair. Someone else grabbed his leg. Patrick kicked out, and his foot hit someone's face, but he was still held fast. Patrick's eyes nipped with tears as his scalp was pulled hard. But he could see at least he had given Mosi the chance to run past them. Patrick couldn't see him, but he hoped by now he was out of the garage. Then he could run. And he had never seen anyone run as fast as Mosi. They would never catch him.

He felt a punch to his side that took his breath away, then the boy with the machete lifted him up and over his shoulder and threw him against the wall.

He cracked against the ground, looked up and realised that now they had no Mosi, they had turned all their attention on him.

'You're gonny be sorry you did that, Patrick Cleary.' The boy with the machete swung it in the air. There was a glint of steel and something seemed to click in Patrick's head, something he should know, but it didn't matter. Nothing mattered. The boys around him all became dark shadows, he couldn't make out any of their faces. All he could see was the machete as it was lifted high above him.

32

Mosi wanted to run. He tried to. He heard Patrick tumble in the darkness behind him. Heard the triumphant yells of the gang of boys. He was almost through the door. Safe. A few more steps and he would be free of them. But he glanced back into the garage, and he could make out Patrick on the ground, scrambling back against the wall, while the boys surrounded him. He was looking up at them defiantly. He had done this to save him. Braver than he had ever been, he thought, and he knew in that instant, he could never leave him.

No matter what it cost him, he could not leave.

Some instinct took over. Mosi stepped back inside the garage, silent as a panther. He stood straight. Then he took a deep breath, he yelled like a soldier going into battle, and he ran towards them.

He took them by surprise. They all turned as one,

their eyes gleaming white in the dark garage. He gave them no time to think. He swung his leg high and kicked at one of the boys, knocking him to the ground. In the same instant he swivelled round and aimed a fist at another. It hit flesh and bone and the boy screamed and fell backwards. In a flash, Mosi had kicked again, another boy's leg cracked and as the boy stumbled Mosi drove the heel of his hand into the boy's Adam's apple. He let out a scream, but Mosi had already leapt in the air and come down hard on another of the boys, sending him sprawling across the floor. The garage was all shouts and swearing. Mosi dropped to a crouch, grabbed someone's leg and pulled him down, then he was on his feet and a kick sent one of the others to the ground. They were all yelling, trying to understand what was happening. He was too fast for them. It was as if they didn't recognise the small black boy they had been tormenting only a moment ago. Mosi didn't stop. The boy with the machete was on his feet again and coming at him fast. Ready to bring it down on him, slashing this way and that, not caring who he hit. The other boys saw him, rolled out of his way. Mosi leapt away. He swung himself round and punched hard into the small of the boy's back, heard the breath pulled from his body. Mosi kicked his legs from under him, and the boy collapsed face down. In the same split second Mosi snatched at the machete, and pulled it from his hands.

The boy was on the ground. Mosi stood above him. Now he was the one with the machete. He backed away from them, one cool step at a time. The other boys, some standing, some still on the garage floor stared up at Mosi.

He swung the machete in an arc around his head. He twirled it, threw it from one hand to the other. Then he beckoned them towards him with his curled fingers. He didn't say a word. Didn't need to. He held their gaze. 'Any time you're ready,' was what that look said. 'Any time you're ready.'

They stood for a moment, watching him, disbelief and fear flashing across their faces. And then, they turned and ran.

33

Patrick lay back against the wall, his mouth hung open. Had he really seen what he thought he had? It all seemed like a scene from a movie. One second they were coming at him, that slash of steel all he could focus on, and the next . . . It was like a whirlwind. Mosi was suddenly there, leaping and kicking. Swinging his fist into one, then another, bringing them all down. Where had he learned to fight like that?

And then, just when he thought he could not be more amazed, Mosi had snatched at the machete and it had come alive in his hand. He stood, silhouetted against the dim beam of light from the street behind him. He looked as if he'd stepped straight out of a Hollywood movie.

The next thing, JD and the rest were gone, running scared, almost bursting through the broken door, their feet splashing in the puddles, not daring to look back.

Patrick could still hear their footsteps racing into the darkness.

Mosi stood for a moment, straight as an arrow. Patrick couldn't move, couldn't say anything. He still couldn't get himself to stand up or take his eyes from Mosi.

He only jumped when Mosi suddenly threw the machete from his hands as if it had given him an electric shock. He fell into a crouch on the ground, buried his head in his hands and . . . was he crying?

That was what made Patrick move. He crept closer to Mosi. 'You saved my life,' he said.

Mosi didn't answer him. He only clutched at his head as if he was in pain.

'Are you OK, Mosi? Did they hurt you?'

Mosi shook his head and Patrick began to get scared because he couldn't understand what was wrong with Mosi. He had just won a battle, single-handed, against the toughest boys in the neighbourhood. Five against one. He should be whooping with joy.

Patrick would be.

He reached out a hand and touched Mosi's shoulder. 'You were brilliant, Mosi.'

'I shouldn't have done it.' The words came out in a sob. 'I should not have done it.'

'Hey, pal, I could have been sliced and diced there, and you saved me.'

Mosi peered at him through his open fingers.

'But now they will tell everyone how I can fight and then . . .'

Patrick smiled. 'Is that all you're worried about? That bunch telling what happened here? Are you jokin', Mosi? You think that JD and the rest of them are going to broadcast that they were beat by one wee asylum seeker? That they left here running like scared rabbits.' He laughed. 'I don't think you'll have to worry on that score. I mean, there is no way they are going to tell anybody that.'

Mosi drew his hands away from his face. He held Patrick's gaze. 'You are sure about this?'

'I can guarantee it. You will have to watch them from now on . . . but I think they'll be too scared to come near you.'

Mosi let out a long sigh. 'I hope you're right.'

'But I don't understand why you want it to be a secret. You're the best fighter I've ever seen, and you let every-body think you're a coward. I mean . . . where did you ever learn to fight like that, Mosi?'

Was Patrick right? Mosi was thinking. Would those boys be too ashamed to tell? He hoped so. If he still prayed, he would pray for such a thing.

Patrick repeated his question. 'Go on, Mosi. You can trust me. Where did you learn to fight like that?'

Mosi looked hard at him. Could he tell him, tell him something he had told no one else here? He wanted to. But could he trust Patrick, and was it fair to tell him?

And then he saw again the moment when Patrick had his chance to escape. He could have left him to his fate. Mosi would never have fought those boys off. Never have risked them finding out that he could fight. But Patrick had not left him. Instead, Patrick had come rushing back, leaping on them, yelling at Mosi to run to safety. Risking the rage of a gang out of control to save someone who was hardly a friend. True bravery.

He knew in that moment that, in spite of Patrick's jokes and smiles, here was someone he could rely on. Someone he could really trust.

And there, in the black darkness of an old abandoned garage on an estate in Glasgow, Mosi began to tell his story, and take Patrick with him on a journey to the heart of evil.

34

'I was just an ordinary boy once. Back in my home in Somalia, I went to school, I played with my brothers. I worked with my father. We were poor but I was happy. I can remember the day everything changed. I was playing football in my village, my friends and I...' Mosi began his story, his voice soft. So soft, Patrick moved closer beside him to listen.

'My best friend was Asad. He was tall for his age, the best at football. We were laughing so much we didn't hear the lorries coming into the village ... until it was too late. The lorries were full of soldiers and we stood and stared at them. Some of the boys ran away. They were the lucky ones. But not Asad and I. We were fascinated. The soldiers looked so handsome in their uniforms, so brave with their guns slung across their shoulders. We waved at them and they waved back. I thought they were just driving through our village – there was a war going on somewhere, we knew that, but it seemed far away to us.

And then, one of the lorries slowed down. I saw two soldiers reach down for Asad, lift him off his feet and haul him into the lorry with them. He was still smiling, as if it was a game, but that was when I realised what was happening. I could see it in the soldiers' faces. Their smiles disappeared. I became afraid, and it was too late because they had Asad. I called out his name. And I ran, hoping I could drag him free of them.'

'And they took you as well,' Patrick said in a whisper.

'It was the last time I ever saw my . . .' Mosi's voice became a sob as if he could not bear to think of it. 'My village.' It was a moment before he began again.

'The lorries left the village, snatching up other boys as they passed. Mothers and fathers ran from their houses, chasing the lorries, but they had no weapons and the soldiers were well armed. They began shooting into the crowd. I could hear screams and shouts. They pushed me on to the floor of the lorry. One of the soldiers held my head down with his foot. I was too afraid to call out.

'We seemed to drive for miles. When they dragged us

from the lorries it was dark. I saw Asad and tried to run to him, but they held me back. They put us in a line and told us we were soldiers now. One boy, even younger than me, began to cry. A soldier hit him with the butt of his rifle and none of us dared cry after that.

'And that was when I first saw him . . .'

Patrick drew in his breath. 'Mr Okafor?'

'I could see his medals shining in the light from the fires, they made me blink. I could hear his voice. "You have no family now," he told us. "I am your family. I am your papa. You will obey me in all things. And if you do not . . . I will know. Because I am magic. And I know everything." And I believed him. We all believed him. "Remember my name," he told us, and the name alone terrified us. "I am Papa Blood." '

'Papa Blood . . .' The name sent a shiver through Patrick too.

'At first I was a runner. Whenever there was a battle, I ran with ammunition, or water, whatever the soldiers needed at the front.'

'Sounds dangerous,' said Patrick softly. There was a drip somewhere in the dark. It had started to rain again outside.

'Of course it was dangerous. But we were not

important. We were easily replaced. If one of us was killed, another was sent in their place. We had no choice. We could not refuse to fight.' Mosi's voice cracked. 'Two boys tried. They tried to run away. But they were caught and dragged back. They made us all stand to attention and they stood them in front of us. Their hands were tied behind their backs.

'And he came again. Closer this time. He walked among us and I had never been so afraid. I could see his face, the cruelty in his eyes. He said the boys were cowards, and there was only one way to deal with cowards.' Mosi buried his face in his hands again. He said nothing for a moment.

'What did he do to them?' Patrick asked softly.

Mosi shook his head. 'Don't ever ask me to tell you that, Patrick.'

Because Mosi couldn't bear to remember that moment. Remember the terror on those boys' faces, and what Papa Blood did to them.

There, in front of them all.

'No one refused to fight after that. I promised myself I would never risk his anger. After that day I really did become a soldier. I learned to shoot. Though most of the guns were bigger than I was. The first time I fired a

Kalashnikov it threw me halfway into the jungle. But I learned. I learned how to use a machete. I learned how to fight. I had no mercy for anyone. I have done some terrible things, Patrick. Terrible things. But I wanted to survive, and Papa Blood had great magic, and we knew it was true. He knew everything. He could soar like a bird and see us, see if we held back during a battle, know if we tried to run away. He could become anything. The mosquito we brushed from our ear, the snake in the undergrowth. I was terrified of him. We all were.'

Again Mosi went quiet, and Patrick began to think he had finished his story. But after a moment he went on. 'And now, I am going to tell you the worst thing . . . the worst thing ever.' He was silent again, as if he needed to draw on every bit of strength he had to tell Patrick this.

'One day he came, and made us all kneel on the ground. He walked past each of us. He would select three, he said, as an example of his magic. To show us how he got his power. He touched the head of one boy, I saw him tumble to the ground in fear. I kept my head down. He moved on and touched the head of another. I heard the boy scream, "No, no, no," but they dragged him off. And then, and then . . . He was so close to me, I could have reached out my hand and touched him and I prayed to become invisible. I wanted his magic to make me invisible. I prayed for him to choose any other boy but me, any other boy, even my best friend, Asad.'

Mosi stopped. Pressed his knuckles against his lips.

'And it was Asad he chose,' Patrick said, knowing Mosi couldn't bear to speak the words.

'And that is when I knew I wasn't human any longer. I was evil like him.' Mosi couldn't stop the tears now. 'He killed them. He said their deaths would make him more powerful. But it was worse than that, Patrick.'

Patrick drew in a deep breath. He was almost too afraid to listen.

It seemed a long time before Mosi spoke again. 'And then he drank their blood.'

35

Patrick's spine turned to ice. How could Mosi have survived after seeing those things? Patrick had been worried about a vampire on the estate. But this monster was worse than any legend. This was real life.

'Now I understand why you were so scared that night when you saw him. But you're safe now, Mosi. Here.'

Mosi's voice was a whisper. 'Papa Blood has great magic, Patrick. That was what held us all there, terrified of what he would do to us if we disobeyed him. He could soar like a bird, change shapes, become anything he wanted.'

At that second, there was a sound, and a shadow passed across the doorway to the garage. Both boys jumped.

He was coming for them.

Then another shape joined the first. A girl giggling.

The couple moved into a clinch, started kissing. Patrick breathed a sigh of relief. The boy and girl stood for a few moments more, then they moved off again.

'Popular place for that kind of thing,' he whispered to Mosi.

Mosi was pale with fear, and Patrick knew he had seen it too, that shadow, and had thought the same thing as him. In those seconds the monster had come back to get him.

'We've got to get away,' Mosi said.

'There's a boat leaving for South America, is that far enough?'

Mosi turned to him quickly, and a hint of a smile lit his face, just a hint, gone in an instant. 'You always joke, even at a time like this, you can still joke.'

Patrick shrugged. 'Would you prefer me to scream? I think I could manage that as well.'

Mosi shook his head. 'I wish I could be like you.'

'Well, that's a first, somebody wanting to be like me.' But it gave Patrick a good feeling that someone could think that way about him.

They got to their feet, and all the time Patrick was thinking of the story Mosi had told him. The horror of it.

They came out of the garage, checked left and right to see if anyone was watching them and ran on. The rain was coming down like steel spikes now. They stopped for a moment to shelter in a doorway.

'It was him who killed Grady,' Mosi said.

Grady. Patrick imagined his body, torn apart and bloodless. The story of Grady's death was almost legend already. No one would ever believe the truth. But who needed truth when you had imagination?

Patrick bent over, hands on his knees, trying to get his breath back. Mosi stood straight, not out of breath at all. 'You're sure? He'd be risking getting found out if he killed Grady.'

Mosi went on. 'Grady tries to hurt him. Grady dies. Yes, I am sure, Patrick. He would never allow anyone to hurt him, to humiliate him.'

'We've got to go to the cops.'

'Have you been listening to me, Patrick? I can't go to the police. If they find out I'm . . .' He stopped dead as if he was about to say something else. 'I was a boy soldier, if they find out what I've done, they'll send me back. They'll send my parents back. No. I can't go to the police.'

'Well . . . I could go.'

'And say what? You recognised Okafor as a wanted war criminal?'

'I could have seen a photo of him on the internet.'

'There are no photographs of him on the internet. No photos anywhere. That's how he could hide so easily.'

Patrick would not give up. 'I could say I suspect him, I think that he's the one who's been doing all those things around the estate, the cat, the blood. They would have to investigate, wouldn't they?'

Mosi's eyes went wide as footballs. 'You would be in danger then, Patrick. Don't you understand by now how evil this man is?'

'But I'd be given police protection, a new identity.' That sounded exciting. 'Relocated . . . somewhere better than here.'

'Then you would be just like me, Patrick, always afraid he would find you . . . come after you.'

'But how would he find out?' he whispered.

And Mosi sighed. 'Magic ways, Patrick. He knows everything.'

Patrick held up his hands. 'Don't say another word,' he said. Because the picture that came into his mind, one that grew bloodier by the second, was Grady's fate in the cemetery.

149

'But we can't let him get away with this, Mosi. There has to be something we can do.'

The rain was a torrent, the sky grey black. The tower blocks closed around them like mountains. Mosi's voice was as dark as the night. 'I think he will win, Patrick. He always wins.'

36

Patrick tossed and turned all night. Couldn't sleep. In a way, he didn't want to. Sleep brought dreams, nightmares. Vampires wandering the estate, waiting for him in the underpass. In the darkness, clinging to the roof, ready to drop on to him. In the snatches of sleep he did manage, he was wandering the dark streets alone, heading home. He heard the swish of wings behind him and he swivelled round, and there looming above him was Papa Blood, arms wide, bared teeth a flash of steel. And he couldn't get away. No matter how he ran.

Finally, Patrick was too afraid to close his eyes at all. He got out of bed and picked up his laptop. He had to find out about this man.

Papa Blood. He was easy to find. Stories of him were legendary. All Mosi had told him was true. And there was more. The cruelty Mosi couldn't bear to speak of was all there to be read about. Patrick had to put the laptop aside, open his bedroom window for air, sure he was going to be sick. How did Mosi bear it?

And when justice had moved in, Papa Blood had disappeared. No one knew where he had gone. But Mosi knew, and so did Patrick.

He was here.

Patrick stood at his window and looked down over the deserted estate. No one was about. The rain had turned to an eerie mist, early morning light beginning to tinge the edges of the sky.

He was out there somewhere, this Papa Blood. He thought he was safe.

They couldn't let him get away. There had to be a way to get him.

37

Mosi watched for Patrick coming through the school gates. He had told him a dangerous secret, and all night he had worried that he had done the wrong thing. The circle must not be broken, his father had told him. Once it was broken, breached, it would be like a dam bursting. All their secrets would spill out, gush out, and then . . .

Had he made a mistake telling Patrick? Perhaps, first chance he got, he would have phoned his friends, told them all. So Mosi waited next morning, expecting Patrick to stride in with Cody and the others, all of them knowing the truth about him. Cody would believe it. After all, he had beaten Cody's brother.

Patrick walked in alone. His eyes were searching for Mosi and when he saw him he hurried across to him. 'I read about him last night . . . on the internet . . . your

Papa Blood. I couldn't believe the things he'd done. It made me feel sick.'

Mosi's eyes flashed to the school gates. Cody was just coming in. Cody glanced at Mosi and looked away quickly, embarrassed.

'Did his brother tell him what happened?'

'Told you he wouldn't say a word, Mosi. He probably told Cody they just scared you a bit and let you go. But Cody'll be dead embarrassed because he was there and ran away.'

He had hardly finished saying it when Cody called across to Patrick, 'I've got something really weird to tell you.' He called out louder, so everyone would hear, 'I've got something really weird to tell the lot of you.'

Mosi held his breath. He was going to tell them all about him. Patrick had been wrong. Cody was going to tell the whole school how he, Mosi, could fight, could use a machete, and they would all ask how he came to learn such things. He wanted to run then, out through the school gates, but where could he go?

'I'm telling you, Mosi, JD would never tell Cody you beat him. Never.' But Patrick's voice trembled and Mosi knew now he wasn't so sure.

They all began to gather round Cody. Even Hakim and his friends. Cody took a deep breath.

'Something happened to my bro last night,' Cody began.

Mosi heard Patrick's quick intake of breath.

'He was coming home in the middle of the night . . . he'd been out with his mates.' For a second, his guilty glance fell on Mosi, then just as quickly moved away. 'And he heard something coming after him . . . he began to run, and it ran as well. Something was chasing him.'

Hakim asked. 'Some . . . thing?'

Cody nodded. 'He says at first he thought it was whoever killed Grady comin' after him. The cops had told them they better be careful. But . . . and this is the weird bit . . . he couldn't see anybody. He could hear them, hear them breathing, he saw this shadow, but he couldn't *see* anybody.'

Bliss shouted out. 'It was his imagination.'

'No way,' Cody shouted back. 'JD's no' easily scared. He woke me up when he came in, he woke the whole house, and I've never seen my bro like that. He was scared. Really scared. Sweating and shaking. He says whatever it was followed him right into the flats. Just a giant black shadow, he never saw anything else . . . He says he thought it was going to get into the lift wi' him. He could hear it coming closer . . . but the doors shut just in time. He didn't see anything, but he knows what it was.'

'Are you saying what I think you're saying? Are you trying to tell us this vampire we've been hearing about was after your brother?' Hakim turned to his friends and smirked. 'His brother tells almost as good a story as he does.'

Cody leapt towards him. 'It's not a story. It's the truth, butthead.'

Hakim grabbed him. 'Who are you calling butthead?'

Cody began yelling. 'I'm telling you. The vampire was after my brother last night. It definitely was!'

There was a murmur of horrified agreement at that.

'I wouldn't believe anything your brother said.' Hakim hardly had the words out when Cody jumped at him.

'Don't you call my brother a liar!' Hakim fell back, and the two boys were locked together on the ground.

The rest of the pupils gathered round, cheering them on.

Mosi and Patrick stayed back.

'I would say it was JD's imagination, but I don't think he's got any,' Patrick said to Mosi in a soft voice.

Mosi's answer was just as quiet. 'It was Papa Blood after him, making himself invisible. He will go after Grady's gang one by one . . .'

'Unless we stop him, Mosi,' Patrick said.

38

Mrs Telford came charging out of the school entrance as soon as she heard the commotion. They were all ordered into the classroom. Even the boldest of them lowered their eyes away from her steely stare.

She waited till they were all gathered together before she spoke. 'I am ashamed of every one of you.' Her voice was soft, yet firm.

'This school is the one place where there should be no violence, no prejudice. And it will be.' Her voice did become a roar then. 'I will have no fighting in this school.'

Everyone shrank back from her anger. Her eagle eye swept the room. 'You! Hakim!'

Mosi saw Hakim jump. 'I didn't start it, Mrs Telford.'

'Did I ask you to speak! Don't you dare say a word. Do you know how shocked your mother and father would be if I told them how you carry on in this school?'

Hakim gulped. His father was always at the forefront of things, speaking up for the asylum seekers, and both his parents were eager to make a success of living in this country. They wanted Hakim to do well, and were always willing to volunteer for anything that would help the school.

'Sorry, Mrs Telford,' Hakim muttered.

'And as for you, Cody.' Her eyes spiked him. Cody had looked smug when her wrath was directed at Hakim. 'Don't think I don't know about you. And all you get up to.'

'It wasn't me,' Cody said automatically.

'It's always you,' Mrs Telford said. 'Well, for the next two weeks you two boys will have an extra lesson, together, just with me, on diplomacy, friendship and tolerance.'

Her eyes again swept the room. And Mosi was invisible. He melted behind the boy in front, kept his eyes downcast. He had learned to become invisible when he was a fighter. The defiant ones who stared back boldly at the soldiers were picked for front-line duty . . . or torture. One as deadly as the other. He had long ago learned to keep his eyes averted. He looked at no one, and no one looked at him. He was invisible. The only way to survive.

Mrs Telford drew in a deep breath. 'Don't think I haven't heard all the talk about this so-called vampire. There are no such things. I know about the old story. Children whipped up into a frenzy about an imaginary vampire. Well, there was no vampire then, and there isn't one now.' She looked again at Cody. 'Has your brother gone to the police about this incident?' She didn't wait for his answer. 'Because he should. And whatever was after him . . . if anything was . . . it was human and dangerous. Certainly not a vampire. I've never heard such a piece of nonsense! You watch too much television, the whole lot of you. Your minds are filled with stories about zombies and monsters and vampires. And that is all they are. Stories.' Had she finished? They all hoped she had. 'I would give anything to see you using those wild imaginations of yours to do something together for once.'

But Mrs Telford even mentioning the vampire only fuelled more stories. In the dinner hall it was all they talked about. Pupils gathered round the tables. Everyone had a story to tell.

'I woke up last night, and there was something scratching at my window,' one of the boys said.

'If that happened to me, I'd wet myself,' Patrick laughed. 'I'm on the thirteenth floor.'

No one laughed. They were all suddenly serious.

Others said they had seen strange shadows too, moving along the ground behind them, shadows dancing on walls, or passing windows.

'My flat looks right over the cemetery,' another of the boys said. 'And at night when I look down I can see a mist rising, and . . .' The boy's voice became soft. They all held their breaths to listen. 'I can see shadows moving in there. As if the dead have come to life. There's nobody there, but I can see these shadows moving.'

Bliss tutted, determined to be the voice of common sense. 'Come on, that was in a film you saw.'

Cody whispered to his friends. 'What was done to Grady, nobody human could have done that.'

Hakim, at the next table, stopped eating for a second. He turned to Cody. 'What *was* done to Grady? We've heard so many stories. Do you think any of those rumours are true? My father says people make things up.'

'That's because the truth is too awful even for the papers to report.' Cody paused dramatically. 'Mutilated.'

Hakim nodded. 'Yes, I heard that.'

Cody swung his legs over his bench so he was facing

Hakim. 'But no blood. He was completely drained of blood.'

There was a communal gasp. 'I heard that too,' Hakim said, and there was a murmur of agreement. 'So . . . how would you know these things?' Hakim asked Cody.

Cody had a ready answer. 'My dad knows some of the police that were there at the scene.'

That was probably true, Patrick thought. Cody's dad had been arrested by most of them.

'What happened to JD was really weird,' Cody said.

'My mum won't even let me out at night any more,' one of the girls said. 'She reckons there's definitely something out there . . . not someone . . . something . . . and until it's caught, I'm grounded.'

Cody turned to the others, stared at them. 'Did I tell you my granda actually saw it . . . the vampire . . . all those years ago?'

'Yeah, you said.'

Patrick looked around. They were all listening intently, gripped by the story. For once, they weren't blaming each other. They had found something else to blame for all that was happening.

'My dad says that when the vampire was here before it

was trying to get people to rise from their graves,' one of the boys said.

Bliss tutted. 'All that was just rumour.'

Cody was shaking his head. 'Naw, naw, that's true. My granda says the last time, him and some of the other boys were going to paint crosses on the gravestones, but the police came and they didnae get the chance.'

Patrick moved forward. 'Crosses on the gravestones? You mean like graffiti?'

Cody stared at him as if he was daft. 'Naw, no' graffiti. Crosses on the gravestones, it's a well-known fact that stops the dead from rising.'

Patrick stepped back from the crowd. He imagined the sound had been turned off in the canteen. He was thinking, thinking hard, and Patrick didn't do that very often.

In that moment he saw how he could tell the world about Papa Blood.

39

Once the idea took hold of him, he knew there was no time to waste. He pulled Cody aside as they left the dinner hall. 'That was a really good idea your granda had, you know, about painting the crosses on the gravestones. Your granda didn't get the chance, but we could . . . we could go to the cemetery tonight.'

He wanted to make Cody think it was his own idea, not Patrick's, and they were just finishing the job Cody's granda had started.

'You mean . . . just you and me?'

Patrick shook his head, drew Cody closer. 'And the other boys in the gang. We'll all paint crosses on the gravestones.'

Cody's eyes lit up and Patrick knew he had him. The thought was exciting Cody. 'I've got a better idea,' Cody said. 'I'll get everybody to go. Just like before. And there'll be that many of us there that nobody'll know it was us painting the crosses. We won't get the blame.' He gave a little laugh as if he had come up with a brilliant plan.

'Do you think they'll all go?' Patrick said softly.

'I'll get them to go,' Cody said with assurance. He grabbed at Hakim as he passed. 'Are you up for going to the cemetery tonight, Hakim?'

Hakim didn't look too sure. 'The cemetery?'

'You're not scared, are you?'

Hakim snapped back, 'I'm not scared. I bet you are.'

The worst thing to say to Cody. 'Me? You know all that vandalism that goes on at the cemetery? Who do you think helps his brother push them gravestones over? Me! I've been in that cemetery loads of times at night. I'm not scared.'

Patrick could see the thought of a vigil for a vampire excited Hakim as well. 'Might be a laugh,' he said.

'Will we do it, then?' This was Patrick. But he didn't really need to ask. Cody was already on his mobile, contacting his mates in other schools who would join them. And a moment later, Hakim was in a huddle with his friends.

Suddenly, the school was buzzing. They were going on a vampire hunt.

40

'There's something on this estate, and we're gonny find out what it is!' Cody stood on the wall in the playground, speaking as if it had all been his idea. Patrick was happy about that.

Standing beside Cody was Hakim. 'And if they're going, so are we.'

Patrick could feel the excitement build in the crowd. There were shouts and yells. Bliss leapt on the wall.

'This is silly. Going out and looking for a vampire! There's no such thing.'

Now it was Cody's turn to shout. 'It's been done before. And this time we could get him.' He said to Bliss, 'We could all go out together tonight. And get the vampire. Safety in numbers, Bliss.'

And though Bliss blinked and looked uncertain, Patrick could see she was intrigued.

'We're not in any danger, there's too many of us,' Hakim assured them all, 'and we'll all stick together.'

Cody shouted, 'I've texted my mates in the other schools. They're up for it.'

'Mine too,' Hakim called out, holding up his iPhone. 'There will be loads of us.'

There was an excitement among them. And Patrick knew it was like a snowball rolling down a hill. Nothing could stop it now. He felt his heart beat faster. He had started all this, with his talk of a vampire.

'I think we should just leave it be.' Ameira's quiet voice could only just be heard.

Everyone looked at her, surprised. 'The cemetery,' she explained. 'It'll still be a crime scene. Police everywhere. It's a waste of time. They won't let us anywhere near it.'

There was a reluctant murmur of agreement.

'It's a big cemetery, Ameira. Only a wee bit of it is a crime scene.' Cody sounded annoyed. Ameira was spoiling the adventure. 'Are you no' coming?' Cody snapped at her.

Patrick could see that Ameira wanted to refuse, to say no . . . I'm not coming. Cody waited for her answer. Patrick felt the whole school wait. Hakim smiled at her.

'We'll all stick together, Ameira,' he said.

Patrick knew what he was really saying. *I'll stick with you, Ameira*.

Ameira smiled back. 'Of course I'm coming . . . never said I wasn't.'

Nothing was going to stop them. The plan was that they would all go home, but meet up again later at the school gates and make their way en masse to the cemetery. There was a buzz in the air Patrick could almost reach out and touch.

'You're not going there, are you?' Mosi asked him. He had stayed back, as usual, when they'd all been talking. Patrick didn't want him to know anything about it. He wasn't part of the plan. It wasn't safe for Mosi to know. Patrick didn't want him involved. Time enough to tell Mosi about it when it was all over.

Patrick shrugged his shoulders. 'It'll be a laugh.'

Mosi looked puzzled. 'You're up to something,' he said.

Patrick just smiled. 'Maybe.'

'Be careful, Patrick.'

As Mosi moved away, Cody asked, 'That weirdo's not coming?'

And Patrick assured him, 'No, he's not coming.'

'Good thing,' Cody said. 'I told the boys to bring their cans, OK? We'll stop that vampire this time.'

Yes, Patrick thought, and I'll get Okafor. Because he didn't intend to spray crosses on the gravestones. He was going to tell the world that Papa Blood was here. He would spray it on the gravestones, he would spray it on the mausoleums and the walls surrounding the cemetery.

Okafor is Papa Blood.
War Criminal.
He's here.

With so many others there Papa Blood would never know who it was who had written those words.

And even if they brought out the workmen to clean it up, just like the last time, they couldn't do it before the police saw it, before the television cameras captured it, and the message would be relayed to the world, and the world would know. They would investigate Mr Okafor. They would take him in for questioning. They would find out the truth.

Papa Blood was magic. Papa Blood could never be caught.

But he, Patrick Cleary, had found a way of getting him at last.

41

Patrick couldn't believe how many had turned up. They seemed to swarm from every part of the estate.

'We're going to meet the rest of them at the cemetery.' Hakim held up his phone. 'They're already heading there.'

'Is everybody ready?' Cody called out. Taking charge along with Hakim. Patrick was happy to let them. He had too much on his mind thinking of what he had to do when he got to the cemetery. As they walked, more seemed to gather, coming round dark corners, from other blocks, even from other areas. And in spite of the fear eating inside him, Patrick couldn't help but be excited.

They passed some women who called out, 'Where are you lot going?' But they were laughing. They were only kids after all. Nothing to be afraid of. They didn't answer the women. Just kept right on walking. Patrick held tight on to the spray can in his pocket.

'This is really silly.' Bliss came up to him, walked beside him. 'If my mum knew I was here, she'd kill me. I had to lie and say I was at Ameira's. And she's at mine.'

'We're all in the same boat, Bliss. My mum would go spare if she knew I was here.' Which wasn't true of course, his mum would never know. She was out on a date. He hadn't a clue when she would make it home.

Even though there was so many of them, as they neared the cemetery they all became eerily silent. There was a moon, almost full, that now and then seemed to peep out of the heavy clouds.

They spread out along the long wall. Some of them climbed on top and sat there, watching. There was a mist rising inside, fingers of it moving around the gravestones.

Patrick found he was holding his breath. It was like a scene from a movie. Nothing seemed real to him.

'I think we should all go home,' Bliss whispered.

'It's an adventure.' He was trying to convince himself as much as her. 'When do we ever have adventures?'

Hakim came running up then. He was breathless, but it wasn't from the running. 'Me and Cody and some of the others are going inside, are you coming?'

Patrick *had* to go inside, yet he was afraid. Now the moment had come, he wasn't sure he could do it. Could he make this work? 'I'm coming,' he said.

'And why aren't you asking me?' Bliss snapped, her own fear suddenly gone.

Hakim shrugged.

'Because I'm a girl, I suppose. Well, Ameira and I are coming too.'

Patrick saw Ameira's eyes go wide with alarm. But Bliss had her by the arm, and pulled her on. 'Come on, Ameira, we'll show them.'

The girls were the first ones in. They climbed over the wall and into the cemetery, with the boys following close behind them. And it was as if they were moving into another world. So close to the estate and the dual carriageway and yet, here, in this world of the dead, all was silent. The gravestones seemed to loom in the moonlight, and their footsteps crunched on gravel or squelched into the mud.

'Spread out,' Cody whispered.

* * *

172

Patrick was sure he didn't want to spread out too much. He didn't like the idea of being alone here. But when he looked they all seemed too far away to him.

As if on cue the moon was swallowed by clouds. It grew even darker. The lights from the street seemed miles away. A misty rain began to fall. Patrick pulled up the hood of his jacket.

Where had they all gone? Patrick felt isolated. He could hear cars zooming up and down the dual carriageway, but he could hear nothing from his friends. He needed to get this done, but he hadn't realised how afraid he would be. He blinked, trying to figure out where to start. He took the can from his pocket. It trembled in his hand.

Patrick shook the can, bent down to a gravestone and sprayed one circle.

O

What was the name? His mind went blank. Same thing always happened when he had to do a test at school. Nerves deleted everything he thought he knew. It was happening again. He had never felt so nervous.

Okafor . . . yes, it was Okafor . . . O. K. A. . . . He tried to spell it out in his head. Maybe, he thought, he should start with Papa Blood . . . yes, easier to spell.

He began to turn the O into a P when, out of the darkness, a voice shouted, 'There! Look, he's there!'

Patrick swivelled round. The can dropped from his fingers.

He heard Hakim yell, 'I see it!'

Patrick jumped to his feet. And he could swear he saw something too. A flash of movement in the misty rain, passing the gravestones. A giant shadow. What was it? One of the girls screamed. Suddenly everyone was yelling. The noise was taken up by the others who had waited outside the cemetery. There were more yells and screams.

He was sure he too had seen that giant figure in the shadows. He could see people running through the cemetery. Soon they would all be gone. He didn't want to be alone here, but he had to finish what he had started. He had to be quick. He got to his knees again, scrabbled round in the darkness for his spray can. Found it at last. No one would see him here. He was invisible. Even if he only sprayed it on one gravestone, he would not leave till it was done. He was so afraid and he wanted to run too, but he had to do this. He had to tell the world about Okafor. About Papa Blood.

A . . . He couldn't stop his hand from shaking.

He stopped for a moment, took in a deep breath. *Get a hold of yourself, Patrick Cleary. You've got to do this.*

And out of the darkness, as if it had emerged from the grave itself, a hand touched his shoulder.

42

Patrick fell back. His breath sucked from his body. All he could see was a huge black hand with a ring on one of the fingers. A gold ring, with a big shiny diamond in the middle. Patrick looked up slowly. Yet he knew what he would see.

Mr Okafor. Papa Blood.

Looking up at him like this he seemed even more of a giant. He'd never been this close to him before. He'd never known fear like this.

'Are you hiding?' The man's voice was like smoke. Deep and dark. A voice that could breathe fire at any moment.

Patrick couldn't speak. The hand on his shoulder lifted him to his feet. The beam from a distant street-lamp caught the diamond in the ring. Patrick could not take his eyes from it. 'I won't tell them you're here,' the voice said, with an almost smile in it.

A soft voice, a voice to make you trust him, make you believe he was gentle. He held up a plastic bag. 'I've been for some shopping. This is the shortcut home for me.'

He moved out of the shadows, and Patrick looked at his face at last. A face wearing a stupid grin. But Patrick knew the truth now. He was looking at a monster. He saw him as Mosi must have seen him. A monster with magic in him. And then the giant smiled and that smile was scarier than anything else. 'Don't be afraid of me . . . I'm only Mr Okafor.'

Patrick couldn't look at his face any longer. He stared down at his hand, still holding his shoulder, at his ring. Anything. But that face.

Patrick had never been so afraid. He thought of Grady. He'd been alone with him too. This man was a monster and he was alone with him here, in the dark, in a cemetery. Patrick felt his eyes being dragged back to the man's face.

'I know you,' the man said. 'You're the boy who was on the television . . . the boy who saw the suicide. What a terrible thing for you to see.' Was his voice changing? Was the gentleness turning to ice?

Patrick took a step away from him. And in that second Papa Blood saw that Patrick recognised him. That

Patrick knew who he really was. His eyes grew hard, like stone. Patrick felt his fingers begin to tighten on his shoulder. In that same second Patrick turned and bit hard into his hand.

He hadn't expected it and Patrick took the chance to pull himself free, and run as he had never run. Between gravestones, leaping over graves, not looking back. Terrified in the knowledge that, even if he escaped now, the monster knew, knew that he had discovered his secret.

43

Mosi saw Patrick coming. Tearing like the wind across the concourse towards the flats. He'd never seen Patrick run so fast. Something had happened. Mosi had heard the police sirens, and the news had travelled fast in this jungle of high-rises. A kindly neighbour knocking at the door, making sure Mosi was safe and at home, had told them. The police had gone to the cemetery, the neighbour said, scattered the pupils. There were rumours about children gathering to hunt a vampire, just like in the old days, and that they were sure they had seen one in the cemetery.

Mosi couldn't make out Patrick's face. His school hoodie was pulled up over his head. Boys all looked the same like that. But it was Patrick all right. He just knew it.

And then he stopped, looked up, his eyes searching the windows, looking for Mosi.

He caught sight of him, gestured to him with a wave.

He wanted to talk to him. He seemed desperate to talk to him. Patrick had been running as if the Devil himself were after him. Or Papa Blood. What if he had seen Patrick wave, saw Mosi at the window. Mosi stepped back.

But when he dared to look again, the estate was deserted. Even more deserted than usual. The rain was heavier now, the mist like a fog. A solitary dog loped between the flats, and then was gone.

He had to see Patrick, find out what was going on. What had happened.

'I'm going out,' he told his parents as they sat in the living room.

His mother looked alarmed. 'Going out? Tonight?'

He smiled to reassure her. There was nothing to be afraid of. 'Only to the landing. My friend, Patrick, is coming up in the lift. I want to talk to him.'

His father looked puzzled. When had Mosi ever called anyone a friend?

'Patrick Cleary,' Mosi explained. He looked at his mother. 'You said you liked his grandmother.'

She smiled, remembering. 'Ah, yes, a kind woman.'

His father still looked worried. 'You're not going into the night?'

'No, Father, I am not going into the night.'

44

Mosi was waiting at the lift when the doors slid open. Patrick was out of breath, his face drained of any colour. He was covered in sweat. He stumbled from the lift and swept the hood from his head. His red hair was clamped to his scalp. He looked terrified.

Patrick shook his head, too breathless to speak. He leaned against the wall. It was a few moments before he was able to say a word. 'Was he following me?'

'No one was following you, Patrick.' And Mosi could always tell. 'Who do you think was following you?'

He wanted Patrick to answer, the police, or Cody, or even Hakim, but he had the ice-cold feeling in his heart that it was someone else. Only one person could cause such terror. He touched Patrick's arm.

Patrick stared at him. His words came in breathless bursts. 'Okafor . . . Papa Blood . . . He knows I know who he is, Mosi. I was in the cemetery . . . I had a great idea to get him . . . I was going to spray it on the walls, on the gravestones, that Okafor was Papa Blood . . .' He punched the wall in anger. 'I didn't even manage that. He was there . . . he grabbed me . . . I'm sorry, Mosi. I couldn't hide it. He saw by my face that I recognised him. He knows me as well. He said . . . "You're the boy who was on the television. The boy who saw the suicide." He knows who I am, and he knows I recognised him.'

'He saw you writing "Okafor is Papa Blood" on the gravestones?' There was terror in Mosi's voice.

Patrick shook his head. 'No, no, I never got the chance to write anything . . . and he was there . . .'

'Then how could he know you recognised him?'

Patrick wasn't listening. 'I'm going to need police protection or something.' He gripped Mosi's hand. 'I've got to go to the police. Don't worry, I won't bring you into it. I promise.'

'So how are you going to explain to the police that you recognised this man? There are no photographs of him anywhere.'

Patrick was shaking his head. 'I can't think. I'm too scared.'

But Mosi was still puzzled. 'Why should he have

suspected that you knew who he really was? You, a boy from the estate? How could he see that you recognised him?' he asked again.

For a moment, the idea that he might be wrong took hold of Patrick. His face seemed to light up. Mosi saw the hope there. But it only lasted for a second. Then Patrick shook his head.

'No, Mosi, he saw the way I was looking at him. He saw how scared I was. I couldn't hide it.' His voice became a whisper. 'Believe me, Mosi. I saw his face change as soon as he realised I knew who he was. That I knew he was Papa Blood.'

45

'I shouldn't have told you.' Mosi was almost speaking to himself. 'I've put you in danger.'

'Maybe I could go to Bliss's dad,' Patrick was also talking to himself.

'Bliss's dad?'

Patrick nodded. 'Her dad's always helping people on the estate. Advising them of their rights and things like that. He's a nice man. Or maybe I could make an anonymous phone call . . .' His eyes lit up. 'Yeah, an anonymous phone call.'

'He would think it was one of us, one of the refugees from his country. We're the only people who could recognise him, Patrick.'

'But he'd be arrested, Mosi. He'd be in prison.'

'He is magic, Patrick. No prison could hold him.'

Patrick slumped against the wall. He knew that

was true too. 'There's got to be something we can do.'

Mosi held his shoulders, and he said again more sure than ever, 'You must be wrong, Patrick, think about it. Because there is no way a boy like you could recognise him. You've been afraid and you imagined it.'

Patrick was trying to think. He'd been nervous, yes, and at that moment when Papa Blood had touched his shoulder, looked into his eyes, he had been frozen with fear.

Maybe he *was* mistaken. Maybe Mosi was right. How could this man have even thought that Patrick knew who he was? The thought comforted him. He began to breathe more easily. 'You're right. Of course you're right. I was just so scared, Mosi.'

Mosi touched his arm. 'Go home, Patrick. You'll be safe at home. We'll talk about it tomorrow. Decide what we have to do.'

Patrick walked up the three flights to his flat. For once, he hoped his granny was in. She would have made soup. She made the best lentil soup this side of the border. He was suddenly desperate for some. Desperate to be home.

He stopped now and again and listened for noises,

looking down the well of the stairs, watching for a move-ment. But he hadn't been followed. Mosi had assured him of that, and Mosi would know. His fear had made him nervous, that was all. He felt better now. Of course he'd been wrong. The thought comforted him. Tomor-row, him and Mosi would talk about it, find a way to get Papa Blood. The graffiti, he was thinking, was still a good idea. He could still use it. Catch him with graffiti sprayed on the walls of the estate.

The phone buzzing in his pocket made him jump. It was Cody. 'Did you get away OK?' He sounded excited. Didn't wait for Patrick's answer. 'It was dead good, wasn't it? Did you get any crosses done? I only did two, and then somebody shouted they saw something, and everybody was yelling . . .' And then he began to babble on about the police arriving, the chase, till Patrick was laughing too. 'Hakim was running like a mad horse. Legs all over the place. He did a leap over the gates at Parkview and he still didn't stop running. I told him I'm going to put him in for the Olympics . . . it was a brilliant night, wasn't it?'

'Did you really see something?' Patrick wanted to know.

'It was definitely the vampire I saw.' Cody, like his granda, would always say he had seen the vampire.

'Definitely,' he said again. 'Hakim saw something as well. Did you?'

He wanted to say . . . Mr Okafor. He saw Mr Okafor, but he had to think about this. 'I saw something. I think . . . Did anybody get caught?'

'I don't think the police were trying to catch anybody . . . just wanted to . . . erm . . . what's the word?'

'Disperse us.' For some reason the word came easily to Patrick.

'Aye, disperse us. Anyway, we were all running in different directions, they didn't know who to follow.' His voice was an excited giggle, and now Patrick was laughing too. He found he was at his front door. He put the key in the lock, opened the door and stepped inside. Talking to Cody was making him feel better. 'What about Bliss?'

'For a minute I thought she was going to go over and talk to the police and explain things, you know Bliss. But then, Ameira grabbed her and shouted, "Your dad will never understand," and Bliss was away, running like the rest of us. It's the best night I've had in ages. Who says we'll do it again the morrow night?'

'Mrs Telford will have us all chained to the school railings when she finds out.'

Cody dismissed that. 'I don't see how she can be annoyed. She's always saying we should do things together, and we did. Hakim and me had a great time. He's all right, you know.'

'I don't think vampire hunting was what Mrs Telford had in mind.' But Patrick was laughing too.

He was glad Cody had phoned. That call, talking about what had happened, laughing, all put a distance between what he'd seen later, as if it hadn't really happened. And of course, he'd been wrong. He could see that now. Okafor hadn't seen that he recognised him. He certainly hadn't chased him out of the cemetery. Probably just lumbered home with his shopping. His own fear had made him overreact. Yes, that was it.

Anyway, he was safe now. He was home.

46

'Granny?' he called out, but he knew his granny wasn't here. There were no lights on, no smell of her in the flat. Nothing. Patrick walked into the living room and switched on the television to see if there was anything about their adventure on the local news.

But he had missed the news. Would have to wait another hour for the next bulletin. He switched to News 24. They were reporting on a riot in Asia somewhere.

'We had a riot here, pal,' he said to the TV. 'A home-grown one.'

But the reporter wasn't listening. And Patrick didn't want to hear the news. He needed cheering up. He flicked through the channels till he found a horror movie. Now that was more like it. Teenagers being chased by a mad axe man always cheered him up.

The phone rang. It was his granny. 'Good thing you're in. There was trouble on the estate the night.'

'Was there?' he said casually. 'Never heard.'

'Never heard indeed!' You could never get away with a lie to his granny. 'Where's that mother of yours?'

He tried to cover for her. Was she in a bath? Having a nap? Busy in the kitchen making him something special to eat? None of them sounded believable and he hesitated a moment too long.

'She's no' in.'

His granny gave a big sigh. Exasperated. And he wondered then if he could tell his granny about Papa Blood. But in the same second he thought of it, he knew that his magic might get to her too. Even his granny, who was scared of no one, wouldn't be safe.

'As long as you're in,' she said at last. 'Have you done your homework?'

She didn't wait for an answer. Knew he would probably lie anyway. 'I'll phone in the morning. Make sure you're up for school.'

He opened the balcony doors and stood looking out over the estate. He loved living this high up, surveying the world, seeing it spread out in front of him, the people like ants on the ground below. It was raining so hard now he could see nothing. The other flats were shrouded in an eerie mist. It made what he could see look even more atmospheric. He wished, as he'd done so often before, that he could recite the names of the hills. The hills that peeked between the tower blocks on a clear day. He knew nothing. But he could change that, he thought, in a sudden fit of enthusiasm. Tomorrow he would learn them. He would make a goal of learning things. Something new every day.

But he couldn't keep Papa Blood's face out of his mind for long. He saw it again, saw his face change from that of a simpleton, to the man who had terrified Mosi. He saw again that flash in his eyes, when he saw that Patrick knew who he really was. Saw the cruel coldness in them.

Yet, Mosi was right, how could Patrick know that? He'd been wrong. Of course, he'd been wrong. That thought lifted his spirits. Yes, that was it. He'd been so scared he'd imagined something that wasn't there.

In his mind he played out that scene in the cemetery again and again. The hand on his shoulder that seemed to come from nowhere, the diamond in his ring catching the light, his voice soft as smoke. *You're the boy who was on the television. The boy who saw that suicide.* Still smiling, till he saw that Patrick had shrunk back, had recognised him. And, yes, that was when his look had changed. That was when those eyes had turned to ice.

The scene played over and over in his mind. The hand on his shoulder, the ring shining in the light, that voice, those eyes. There was something here that was knocking on his memory. But what was it?

The diamond in Papa Blood's ring catching the light . . .

And in a flash, another scene was being played out in front of Patrick's eyes. His legs went weak. And he knew he was in even more danger.

47

Mosi sat in his bedroom. Patrick had been wrong. Papa Blood had not realised that he recognised him. That was impossible. Had to be impossible.

From the living room he heard his mother laugh at something on television and her laugh made him smile. His mother laughed so rarely. He had to protect his parents. They had risked everything to keep him safe. Everything.

But perhaps now it was time to face up to his past too. He had to protect Patrick.

If only he had not told Patrick about Papa Blood.

It was all Mosi's fault.

And yet . . .

His head ached trying to work this out. Something gnawed at his brain. Patrick had been so sure. What if he was right? That Papa Blood sensed that Patrick knew his real identity? Why should he think that look of recognition meant Patrick knew his real identity?

Unless . . .

He held his head between his hands as if he could take control of the thoughts tumbling in his mind.

Unless he thought that Patrick had recognised him, not as Papa Blood, but as someone else? And what had he said to Patrick? *You're the boy who was on the television. The boy who saw the suicide.*

Hassan, that man who had died, had been terrified of something. Afraid of being sent back, they all said. He had been nervous and afraid for weeks, people said. Stocking up an empty flat to hide in. When his brother had disappeared, he had become even more afraid.

But, what if he had been afraid not of being sent back, but of something else? Someone else.

Papa Blood.

What if Hassan, and his brother, had recognised Okafor as Papa Blood too.

Mosi shot forward. He lost control of his thoughts completely.

Mosi remembered the dead cat in the underpass. The blood smeared over the graffiti. Why didn't he realise it before? They had all been warnings. Warnings to anyone who might have recognised him here.

A warning to Hassan, and his brother.

But Papa Blood had taken no chances. He had found Hassan. It hadn't been a suicide at the top of that tower block. It had been murder.

And Patrick had seen it.

48

Patrick's head was swimming. He felt dizzy. The memory of that day played in his head like a scene from a film. It had been a murder he had witnessed. How could he not have realised that before? The first thing that had caught his eye, that tiny beam of light, for a second dancing along the wall. Now, he realised what it had been. It had been the light flashing from that big diamond in Okafor's ring. He saw again all that had happened on that rooftop. He couldn't get it out of his head.

That moment came spinning into his mind once more. A memory locked away until he had seen the flash from Okafor's ring and it had suddenly come flooding back. Now Patrick was returned to that morning, He was waiting at the lift, when, just for a second, a dancing beam of light had caught his eye, and he had turned and seen the man falling, his arms flailing wildly, as if he was trying to hold on to something. Hadn't he thought then that the man must have changed his mind? But he hadn't changed his mind. He'd never wanted to jump in the first place. He wanted to live. Patrick's eyes hadn't followed his descent to the ground. He couldn't bear to look at that. Instead, he had moved his eyes back to the roof and he had seen someone else there. Someone who moved out of view at the same moment the man had gone over the edge.

But Patrick had seen that person. Even now, he could see clearly who it was.

Mr Okafor. Papa Blood.

And Okafor had looked across and seen Patrick watching him. For a second their eyes had locked. That was the recognition he had seen in Patrick's eyes. Not that he was Papa Blood, hiding here under a false identity, but that here was the man responsible for Hassan's death.

Patrick's brain went into overdrive. He saw now how they could catch Papa Blood. And keep Mosi out of it. If Patrick went to the police and told them he'd seen Mr Okafor at the scene of the crime, surely they would take Mr Okafor in for questioning, and once in custody they would take his fingerprints, his DNA, whatever, and they would find out his true identity.

Nothing to do with Mosi.

He punched the air with satisfaction.

He should tell the police now. He almost reached for the phone, but no. He wanted to tell Mosi. He wanted him to know he was safe. He, Patrick, had worked it out. He, Patrick, had saved the day. He wanted to go down and tell Mosi. See the look on his face.

He took a step, and just then, he heard a squeak of a floorboard in the hall.

Someone was in the flat with him.

49

Patrick prayed it was his mum. He wanted to call out, but he had no voice. Because he knew in his heart it wasn't her. His mum would have bounced in, yapping loudly, the moment she came through the door. No. It wasn't his mother.

It was Papa Blood. But how had he got in?

Patrick wondered with a shiver of fear if he'd left the door on the latch. Always getting into trouble for it, and had he done it again, on the phone to Cody, not thinking? That stupid mistake might cost him his . . .

No. Don't think like that, Patrick.

He looked around for a place to hide. A place to escape. But there was none. There was only this room, with the kitchen off it and he wouldn't have time to make it in there.

He was on the thirteenth floor of a tower block. Thirteen floors up. Thirteen floors down.

Another squeak. He could hear it above the noise of the horror movie. The only light in the room its flickering images on the wall.

He could scream at the top of his lungs, alert the whole estate, but they'd only think it was the movie. The volume too loud. He wanted to switch it off.

Why couldn't his body move?

A weapon. He needed a weapon. His eyes darted round the room. In films there was always something handy.

If he could make it to the kitchen, there would be a knife. But he would never make it to the kitchen.

Another squeak. And the memory bore itself into his head, what Mosi had told him, or hadn't told him. What Papa Blood had done to those boys. Something so bad Mosi couldn't bring himself even to speak of it. The horrors Patrick had read on the internet flooded back to him. His limbs unfroze and his brain started working again.

His mum, as usual, hadn't cleared up the tea dishes. His plate and hers were still lying on the sofa. And crossed over them, two forks, two knives. Steak knives. He snatched both knives up from the plates. And moved as silently as he could behind the door.

The shadow loomed against the wall. A scream went up from the television, Patrick began to sweat.

One more step, Papa Blood was almost inside the room. This was his chance. Surprise was his only other weapon. Patrick leapt at him, struck as hard as he could, but Papa Blood was a giant and one knife seemed to bounce off his chest. The other sank into his arm. He plucked it out and threw it aside. But the blow was enough to make him stagger back for a moment. Patrick snatched his chance and tried to get past him, making for the front door. But Papa Blood grabbed him and brought him down. Patrick kicked hard at his face, rolled away and got to his feet again.

Papa Blood made no sound. No shout. No yell. Used to tackling an enemy in silent darkness.

The only sound was from the television. Screams and yells, teenagers running from some unreal horror. Some kind of cloaked monster coming after them.

Papa Blood was on his feet too.

Patrick made a run for the open balcony door. 'Help!' he screamed it out into the night. 'Help!!!!' As loud as he could.

A dying teenager screamed in the movie.

A big hand clasped over his mouth and he was dragged

back. Patrick sank his teeth hard into Papa Blood's hand. For a half-second he let go and Patrick twisted away, tried to go past him. But he was grabbed again and lifted off his feet. Patrick knew what he intended.

He was lifting him towards the balcony. This would be another tragic accident, or a teenage suicide.

The terror of it gave Patrick strength he didn't know he had. He kicked his legs wildly. He reached for the edge of the balcony door, curled his fingers round it.

'No!' He yelled it out but it was drowned in the noise from the film. He had to hold on. That thought was steel in his head. Hold on! He would not let go of that door, nothing would make him loosen his grip, because as soon as he did, it would be all over for him.

And with one swoop Papa Blood brought down his giant fist on Patrick's arm. He heard the crack. The sudden blast of pain almost made him faint. But he couldn't faint. He let go, no choice, and his arm fell uselessly against him. He felt himself being lifted, and he knew he was going over. And he couldn't do anything to stop it.

And right then, another figure leapt out of the darkness. It was Mosi.

He was swinging a baseball bat wildly and moving so

fast he gave Papa Blood no time to think. Papa Blood dropped Patrick to the ground, and turned on Mosi. But Mosi was too fast for him. He swung the bat at Papa Blood's chest, and again and again, pushing him back against the low balcony wall. The man began to lose his balance. He tried to right himself, but again Mosi gave him no chance. He cracked the bat against Papa Blood's head and he tumbled right back, his hands reaching for something to stop him, but there was nothing. And with a grunt, just a grunt, he went over the wall and into the darkness beyond.

50

'Is he dead?' Patrick's voice was thick with pain. He wanted to pass out. 'Is he dead, Mosi?'

Mosi let the bat slip from his shaking hands. He turned to Patrick but he said nothing.

'He must be dead. Look and see, Mosi. Look over and see.'

'He's gone, Patrick,' Mosi said, he sounded as if he might cry. 'Is your arm broken? You need help.'

Patrick tried to answer, but it hurt to speak. Then in an instant the words would not come. Because he could see what Mosi couldn't. Behind him fingers appearing again above the balcony, the hand clutching at the wall, pulling itself up.

'Mosi . . .'

His frightened eyes told Mosi everything. Mosi swung round. He could see the face, Papa Blood's face, so close, so terrifying. He shook with fear when he saw those eyes.

Was this man immortal? Would he never die?

'Help me . . .' His fingers clawed at the top of the wall. One foot rested on a ledge below. Beneath him the ground disappeared into murky, misty darkness.

'*I caaw,*' he said again, in their own language. Pleading with him as if that would make a difference.

And all Mosi would have to do was press on those fingers and Papa Blood would lose his grip. He would fall. He would die at last. All he had to do was push against that terrifying face that had never shown pity for anyone. One simple push, and the monster would fall.

He had the power to end it, to kill him, to let him die. To avenge Asad, and all the others. Justice would be served.

And he couldn't do it.

Mosi reached down for his hand.

Patrick's voice behind him. 'What are you doing, Mosi!' Unbelieving.

The big hand folded itself around his. Squeezed. Was that with gratitude? Mosi knew he could never haul him up, but he could help him get a good grip on the balcony wall. Then he would leave him there, get Patrick, get them both out of here as quickly as he could. Alert the police. Papa Blood would be arrested for Hassan's murder. Mosi had no thought in his head but that. But he could not push him over.

Papa Blood lost his footing on the ledge. Now, the only thing holding him was Mosi. He tried desperately to get a footing on the ledge again, but it was impossible. His foot was wet, the ledge was slippery. And Mosi knew he was not strong enough to haul him up, or hold him for much longer.

Papa Blood knew that too. His eyes changed. The squeeze on Mosi's fingers became more painful. Mosi realised too late what Papa Blood was doing. If he was going down, he wasn't going down alone.

Mosi tried to pull his hand free, but the grip was tight. Papa Blood's eyes didn't leave him. His face was twisted into a snarl. Mosi's foot slipped on the wet balcony. He began to lose his balance. He struggled, and his foot slipped again. The man's hand was too strong, his grip too fierce.

In that instant he was back in Africa, and Papa Blood was there in front of him, in front of them all. He could still hear his words. *You can never escape from Papa Blood.*

And in that second Mosi knew he was right. He would never get away from him.

The thought was too much to bear. Mosi closed his eyes and prayed, and he had not prayed in such a long time.

In that same moment, Papa Blood's wet hand began to slide from Mosi's grasp. Papa Blood's eyes grew wide. Was he afraid? No. He didn't look afraid. Just angry. Angry because he knew there was no saving him now.

Finger by finger his hand slipped free and Mosi watched him go, falling back, his arms waving wildly. His voice a wailing howl in the night.

Down and down and down.

Mosi stepped back before he hit the ground. Stepped back and slid to the ground beside Patrick.

'I can't believe you, Mosi.' Patrick's voice was weak, his face white as a corpse. 'You tried to save him, Mosi. He was going to kill the both of us, and you were trying to save him.'

How could he explain? How could he tell him? 'I made a promise, Patrick, long ago. I will never kill anyone else in my life. Not deliberately. No matter what, I will never kill again.'

51

'Hey, son, are you OK?'

The sudden call wafted from the mist surrounding the tower block opposite. A man's voice, almost panicking. 'Son! Are you OK!'

Mosi drew in his breath. 'Someone saw me. Someone was watching!'

Patrick struggled to his feet. 'Go, Mosi. Go right now.' Then he waved across at the man with his one good arm while the other hung limply.

'I'm OK . . . call the police!'

'Done!' the man shouted and through the mist Patrick could see him waving a mobile phone.

Patrick was almost afraid to look down. Too afraid that there would be no body there, that the concourse would be empty. Didn't that always happen in the horror movies he loved so much? The body disappears only to come back in the sequel and kill again.

He did look. The mist was too thick to see that far down. But he could hear the yells, the shouts, as people were gathering there. More people were coming out on to their balconies.

'You've got to go now, Mosi,' he said. 'Keep out of this.' There would be people coming to his flat soon. 'Hurry.'

Mosi got to his feet. He backed into the flat. He looked almost as pale as Patrick. 'But that man saw me from his balcony.'

Patrick was thinking fast. 'I can hardly make him out in this rain. He saw a boy. We're both wearing school hoodies, we all look the same. And it's dark and misty, he won't have seen much else. I'll say it was me.' Blackness was swimming in front of his eyes. It was hard to keep talking. 'They can't find you here.'

Mosi seemed to be fading down a long tunnel. He was saying something, but Patrick could hardly make out what it was. His voice coming from somewhere far away.

Patrick was so frightened he would be caught. 'Go, Mosi. They'll be here soon . . .'

There was a sound at the door. Someone was here already. No time for escape.

'The cupboard in the hall, Mosi, hide in there . . . get out when you can.' Mosi's flat had the same cupboard. Mosi ran for it. Stopped for a moment at the door. 'Thank you, Patrick.'

The door was knocked again. In a second they would realise it was on the latch and come right in.

Patrick wanted to say something, but the pain was too much and he felt blackness closing in on him. 'Go, Mosi,' was all he managed to say. He waited till Mosi was safely inside the hall cupboard, till he heard the door click closed, only then did he call out weakly . . . 'I'm in here . . .' He heard the footsteps running up the hall. Voices calling him. It seemed to him the room grew darker and darker, and he slumped to the floor.

52

Patrick was drifting in and out of consciousness. He would open his eyes to try to make out who was there, but the picture was fuzzy, the faces crowded round him smudged, and the people were speaking as if they were in a badly dubbed film.

'The ambulance's coming.'

'His arm's broken.'

'Where's his mother?'

He wanted to tell them everything, but his lips seemed to be glued together. A spasm of pain made him moan and the blackness wrapped itself around him again.

How long he was unconscious he didn't know but when he opened his eyes the paramedics were there, hovering over him.

'Give the boy some breathing space.'

'We're giving you an injection for the pain, son.'

And then a face, a voice. 'I saw it all. That wee boy is a hero. That big guy trying to chuck him over the balcony . . . I couldn't believe what I was seeing, and it was him that went over instead, thank God. Big guy, lost his balance, must have slipped on the wet tiles. Over he went, still clinging on for grim death and then, that wee boy there!' The man's face seemed to zoom closer. 'He was on his feet and trying to help him. Trying to pull him up and him with a broken arm.'

The faces turned to him, looking at him as if he'd changed in some way. He wasn't an ordinary boy any longer.

He was a hero.

Patrick began to shake his head. He wanted to tell them. No, it wasn't him. He wasn't the hero. He would have let him drop. It was Mosi who was the hero.

But the words wouldn't come and the pain was easing and he slipped back into unconsciousness again.

It was so easy to step unseen from the cupboard. People were filling the flat, but they were all in the living room. And even if he was spotted he was just a boy who had come to see that Patrick was OK, to check on his school friend.

But no one saw him. He left as soon as he could, passing the paramedics rushing into the flat. As he hurried down the stairs to his own flat he looked for a moment out of the landing window. It was alive down there on the ground. There were police cars, ambulances, blue lights flashing, people crowding round.

Papa Blood was dead. Mosi had escaped him. He need fear no longer. He would tell his father and mother all that had happened when he got home. Safe to tell them now.

What had made him go then to Patrick's? Choose that moment? A few seconds later and he would have been too late. Patrick would have been dead.

Something had brought him to Patrick's home.

Something stronger than witchcraft.

Something more powerful than magic.

And in that moment Mosi got his faith back.

And it felt good.

53

When he'd come out of hospital Patrick had discovered that he wasn't the only hero. Hakim was sharing in his glory.

Because in the end it wasn't fingerprints or DNA that gave up Papa Blood's true identity, though they would have before long. It was all down to Hakim's iPhone. He had caught Papa Blood on video in the cemetery that night and had posted it on YouTube. Seen by half the world, someone, somewhere had recognised him for what he really was. Papa Blood, a cruel warlord, the world's most wanted.

Patrick and Mosi were sitting on a wall beside the football pitch. Patrick's arm was still in plaster. It had been a bad break. 'I will never play the piano again,' he had told Bliss when she'd come to visit him.

Her answer had been typical. 'You never played it before.'

'Lucky break, then, eh?'

Still making a joke about everything.

'Lucky break, eh? Get it?'

It was a bit annoying though that Hakim was getting almost as much attention as Patrick. 'Hakim's walking about as if he's superman. As if he's the one who exposed Mr Okafor as Papa Blood.'

Mosi shrugged. 'That's not a lie. It was his video on YouTube that did it.'

'He wouldn't have been taking the video at all, if it hadn't been for me.'

'Well, you're a hero too,' Mosi said.

Patrick stared at him. 'Are you winding me up? You know I feel guilty about that.' His voice became a whisper. 'You're the hero, Mosi. And nobody knows it. Nobody knows you had anything to do with Papa Blood. You kept well out of everything. You really did stay invisible, Mosi.'

Mosi smiled. 'I am free of Papa Blood and that is all the reward I want.'

And he had felt it these past few days. He and his parents had smiled more often.

It had been discovered that Papa Blood had been here on someone else's passport. Mr Okafor, the real gentle giant, had been murdered by him.

'That ring belonged to the real Mr Okafor, did you read that?' Patrick said, not for the first time. 'And it was the ring that gave him away . . . do you not think that's funny. The Lord works in mysterious ways, my granny says.'

'My mother says the same thing, Patrick,' Mosi said.

'It's over, Mosi. You're safe.'

Mosi nodded. 'Things will be better now, Patrick.'

'Do you think so?' Patrick didn't sound so sure. 'My granny's decided to move in with us. No more getting out at night-time . . . for me or my mum. We're both grounded. She's driving us mad. She's even teaching my mum to cook.' He made a face. 'Don't ever taste my mum's cooking if you want to make it out alive.'

Mosi smiled. Patrick always made him laugh.

'Me and Mum are trying to think up ways to get rid of her. I suggested giving her a plate of my mother's soup. That would poison anybody. Failing that, I think my mother should get another man. A new daddy for me. Eh, what do you think?'

A ball dribbled to a halt in front of them. One of the boys on the pitch, Brian, shouted over, 'Hey, kick it back.'

Patrick held up his arm. 'Wounded soldier here. I cannae do it.'

And Mosi, for the first time since the day he was taken by the soldiers, took aim and kicked the ball high. The boy caught it with his foot and called back, 'Want a game?'

He beckoned Mosi over.

Patrick grinned at him. 'On you go. I'll sit here and watch. I need a laugh.'

And Mosi ran on to the pitch.

And joined the game.

The Fact Behind the Fiction

One of the amazing things about *Mosi's War* is that the inspiration for it partly came from a true story. In 1954 there were rumours of a vampire roaming the Necropolis, a large cemetery in Glasgow – a seven-foot vampire with iron teeth. Hundreds of children, aged from four to fourteen, were so convinced there was a vampire that they decided to try to trap it in the cemetery. There was a stampede when many of them thought they had seen the vampire wandering in the darkness. The police came and dispersed the children. Teachers assured them there was no vampire. But they came back night after night.

The vampire was even discussed in Parliament, and this led to the banning of American horror comics, thought to be the cause of the mass hysteria among the children.

The story died, but there were many who thought the

vampire had only disappeared, and one day he would come back to have his revenge.

In real life, though, there are worse things than vampires . . . War criminals, just like Papa Blood, are hiding throughout the world under false identities, and they are the ones who should be exposed and brought to justice.

You never betray your friends.
And you definitely don't snitch on gang leaders.
Not unless you don't value your life – like Sharkey.

Read on for a taste of another gripping thriller
by Cathy MacPhail . . .

'Want a Mint Imperial?' I handed over the bag of my favourite sweets to my mate, Sean.

He pushed it back at me, and pulled a Mars bar from his pocket. 'You know I hate them things, Leo. Gimme chocolate any day.'

We were on the train heading home after the Saturday match. Our team had lost 3–0, but in our minds we had not been defeated. We usually lost by a lot more than that. Nearly all our friends supported Rangers or Celtic. But not me and Sean. We liked to be different. We were Barnhill men, like our dads before us. We supported our local team, Barnhill. Or, 'Barnhill Nil', as some rotten people liked to call them.

We were well pleased that day as we headed home on the coastal railway line past Dumbarton Rock, watching the river sunset red and the whole town bathed in a pink glow.

'We're really lucky living in the best place in the world, with the best football team.'

Sean laughed. He agreed with me. 'When they were handing out luck, McCabe, God gave us an extra share.'

That's how me and Sean always were. We agreed about everything. We were best mates. Had been since Primary 1. We liked the same things . . . except when it came to Mint Imperials – but then you can't have everything.

We were just drawing into one of the stations when Sean pointed towards a wall surrounding one of the derelict factories. 'Hey, look at that.'

It would have been hard to miss what was written on that wall. Painted in giant whitewashed letters.

SHARKEY IS A GRASS

I hadn't a clue who Sharkey was, but I knew one thing. 'Sharkey's a dead man,' I said. 'They should have added RIP – Rest in Peace.'

'Or rest in pieces.' Sean laughed. ''Cause they'll probably cut him up and drop his body bit by bit into the Clyde.'

Me and Sean are big C.S.I. fans and they'd had a storyline just like that only a couple of weeks ago.

'I wonder who Sharkey grassed on?' I said.

'Could have been Nelis, or Armour, or McCrae.'

Everyone knew the top gang leaders in the town. The drug dealers, the hard men, the bad men. Nelis had an evil reputation for doing the most awful things, and Armour was simply called 'The Man'. As if there was no other. McCrae was vile. His name would always be linked to the Sheridan lassie. She'd come from a decent family but once she'd started running about with McCrae he'd got her on to drugs. Her life had spiralled downhill, and when she'd finally had the courage to leave him she'd been found shot dead not far from McCrae's house. No one leaves McCrae. He had even been charged with her murder but managed to get off when two of his 'friends' had supplied him with an alibi. But no one doubted his guilt. Andy Sheridan, the girl's dad, had sworn all kinds of vengeance on him for that.

McCrae and the others always got off due to lack of evidence – or lack of surviving witnesses. No one ever grassed on them because once you did you'd be a dead man, like Sharkey would be soon.

'He's probably left town already,' Sean said.

But Sharkey, whoever he was, the drug dealers, the crime bosses, everything was forgotten by the time the train stopped at our station. We were going to Sean's house. He had a new PlayStation game and we were dying to try it out.

Sean lived in McCrae territory. Crazy, I know, that they claimed areas of the town as their own, but that was the way it was. Sean and me, we were streetwise enough to know that. But we kept back from any trouble. My dad and Sean's would have gone spare if they'd caught us having dealings with anyone connected to McCrae or any of the others.

And on the way to Sean's house we did what we loved best. We explored.

The area where Sean lived had so many boarded-up houses and derelict properties and shops, and me and Sean were experts at getting inside them. It was exciting and a bit dangerous as well. You never knew what you might find. It was about the only risky thing we did and it didn't hurt anybody. We'd sneak inside, pretend we were SAS commandos searching out terrorists, or crime scene investigators looking for clues. Always the good guys, me and Sean.

There was a new boarded-up shop to explore that

night. Azam had finally had enough. He'd given up after all the hold-ups and break-ins and vandalism to his shop. He had closed up and decided to move to somewhere less dangerous. 'Baghdad, I think,' he had told Sean's dad. 'It's a lot safer there.'

'My dad says it was a blinkin' shame,' Sean said. 'Azam was trying to give the people here a good corner-shop service. They never gave him a chance.'

It sounded like something Sean's dad would say. Like my dad, Sean's was always complaining about how the town was run by those three gang bosses.

'If Azam had paid McCrae protection money, he could have stayed,' I said to Sean. And he agreed. Everyone knew it went on. McCrae would threaten the small shopkeepers with his gang of hard men, who would break up the shop or warn customers to stay away – shop somewhere else. In the end most of the shopkeepers would pay up just for the sake of peace. But after that they would be in McCrae's pocket for ever.

'The Untouchables', my dad called Nelis and Armour and McCrae. Because the law could never seem to touch them. They got off with everything. Verdicts not guilty, or not proven.

So now Azam's once brightly whitewashed shop was

covered in graffiti – on the walls, on the door. Even on the steel panels that boarded up the windows. It was easy getting inside. Me and Sean were experts at finding a way. One of those steel panels was lying askew at the back door, and first me and then Sean squeezed through. First thing that hit us was the smell. Somebody had been using this place as a toilet.

Sean started dancing about like a cat on a sizzling hob unit. 'Hope I don't put my feet on something yucky.'

I was almost tempted to squeeze back through into the street, but my crime-busting instincts took over. I pulled out the pen-torch I carried with me (well, I did say we were always exploring) and flashed it across the ground. Just as well. Another few steps and Sean *would* have stepped on something yucky. The vandals had obviously been here already. It never took long for them to get inside any derelict properties. There was broken glass all over the floor, pipes had been ripped from the walls. There was graffiti on every empty space.

'I hear something,' Sean said.

I could hear it too. A low moan from one of the dark corners. We were always hoping to find evidence of a crime or a robbery in progress, maybe stumble across the aftermath of mayhem – a dismembered body in black bin bags strewn across the floor. So far the only thing we'd ever come across was a gold watch. We took it to the police. Got a reward too. Didn't I say we were always the good guys, me and Sean?

But here in the dark, listening to that moaning coming from the shadows, it occurred to me that right at this minute I'd rather be at Sean's playing his new Zombie computer game.

Neither of us moved. The moan became a growl. I flashed my torch towards the sound.

I thought at first it was a wild animal. All hair and teeth. It leapt at us. Me and Sean yelled and this time Sean didn't miss the yucky stuff. He sank his foot right in it.

The face became clear. It was an old man, a dosser. He was yelling like a beast.

'Get oota my place! Ya wee . . .' He threw something at us. We didn't wait to find out what it was. We had never moved so fast, squeezing out of the door almost at the same time. It was only as we were running away that we started to laugh. Laugh until we couldn't stop.

'Oh, we would be brilliant crime scene investigators,' I said. 'One old weirdo and we're off faster than a speeding bullet.'

I made a whizzing sound, and it only made us laugh all the more.

My dad picked me up later at Sean's. My dad nearly always picked me up . . . or my mum did.

'I'm not having my boy walking these streets late at night,' they would both say.

I had a great mum and dad. A great family and the best mate in the world. Sean.

That night as my dad was driving me home and I was yattering on about the match – giving him a kick-by-kick description of the game – I was really happy. Life was good.

Nothing was ever going to change that.

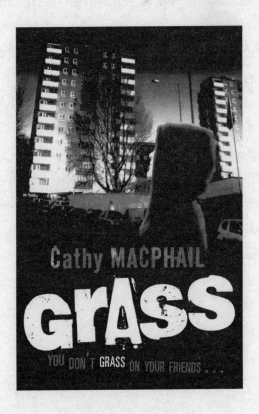

The world's greatest secrets are in danger of
falling into the wrong hands. It's down to renegades
Jake and Lauren to find them . . . before it's too late.

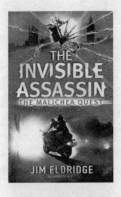

Don't miss out on four action-packed thrillers,
full of danger and conspiracy

www.bloomsbury.com
www.jimeldridge.com
Hooked on Books